HONEY DRIPPING HEART THROB

BAKE SALE BACHELORS SEASON THREE,
BOOK SIX

AVA BERINGER

Get FREE short stories when you sign up for my newsletter!

1

CHRIS

"Isabella, we talked about this," I said in my flirtiest, gentlest tone. I tilted my head and lifted my eyebrows at the face on my phone screen, a gorgeous alpha woman who was so full of charm that she wasn't used to hearing "no" for an answer. "We had a good time, but we both agreed that was it."

Isabella smoothed her thumb and forefinger down her chin and licked her lips, her tongue rolling smoothly over her "r's" in her lightly-accented English. "I know what we *said*, but that was in the past. Rules are made to be broken, sexy."

She wasn't the first to try for more, and she wouldn't be the last. To be honest, lately, I'd been thinking about having *more* with somebody special. It just didn't seem realistic. There wasn't any special someone out there waiting for me, and even if there was, I wouldn't be able to commit. I rolled my eyes playfully as I crossed from my stove top to my kitchen island. "Not this time, sharpshooter."

"Are you sure?"

She was distracting me from the dinner I was cooking with

her sexy looks and rolling "r". Well, trying to cook, since I wasn't much of one. I cut my eyes to the sizzling skillet, which let up steam and a savory aroma. It seemed okay for now. "Yes, I'm sure."

She chuckled and shrugged a shoulder. "It was worth a shot, wasn't it?"

"Can't say I blame you," I replied, using a hand to motion toward my whole being. She laughed out loud. She was a sexy, confident, seductive alpha. Lots of fun and lots of mystique. That's how I wanted to keep it in my memories. "It really was fun, though. Take care, alright?"

Isabella wasn't fazed. We both knew how these things went. "You do the same, doctor. Goodbye."

I clicked off the line. At the same time, my phone danced on the granite countertop, blinking with a text message. It was from Martrice, a thoracic surgeon I met at a conference in Atlanta.

In town. Let's meet. The winky face and tongue out emoji told me exactly what she wanted to meet for. Like most of the alphas I met she didn't ask, just assumed I'd say yes in the typical cat and mouse game I played with them. I always won.

We'd been together twice. I tilted my head back and forth, debating whether or not I wanted to go for the third and final time with her.

I typed, *Looking for another lesson in building dexterity in your fingers?*

Her answer came almost immediately, phone shaking in my palm. *While it is top-notch, I'm always looking for ways to up my game, doctor.* Along with that came a picture of her puckered lips, thick and lacquered red, one fingertip in between them, resting on the tip of her tongue. I shivered, remembering our last night together. We'd both taught each other some tricks. I wasn't interested in another performance, though. We'd had our fun, and lately the "hit and runs" just weren't as alluring as they used to be. *Because you want to settle down,* came a quiet voice in the back of my mind. So quiet, I acted like it wasn't there.

I smelled burning. When I wheeled around plumes of brown, angry-looking smoke floated up from the cast-iron skillet on the range.

"Shit," I muttered. "My filets." I was supposed to sear the outsides, then put them in the oven. "Forget seared, these are blackened." I grabbed a pair of blue oven mitts that I'd never even used before and dumped everything in the sink. I turned the faucet on and the water hit the pan with a loud hiss and an angry cloud of grayish-brown steam. "I'll deal with this crap later."

I opened the kitchen window, twenty stories up. The sounds of Philly traffic, with honks coming as often as notes on a sheet of music, wafted up on the cool night air and filled my condo. I sat at my glass dining room table, dropped my elbow on it and my chin in my hand, and sighed. The burnt dinner was minor. The new feeling that something was missing? That was harder to acknowledge. For once, I was not looking forward to dinner in peaceful and quiet solitude. I hated to admit it, but maybe I wanted someone there with me.

Knock, knock, knock. To say I was shocked was an understatement.

I rose slowly from my chair. "Who could that be?" I wasn't expecting anyone, that was for sure. My plan was to cook myself a tasty dinner, relax for the few days I was home in Philly, and review some new suturing techniques in preparation for my next surgery in Clearvale, Minnesota, of all places.

My heart pounded with excitement as I looked through my

peephole. A tall, debonair alpha stood there in a cashmere sweater and slacks, a big, expensive watch shining on his wrist as he casually tucked his hand in his pocket, looking like he just stepped out of GQ magazine. Guy Guillaume, the alpha who I'd broken rules for lately. Had he somehow heard my inner cry of loneliness?

I cracked the door open, putting on a flirtatious smile. "I don't remember extending a dinner invitation, Guy." I pretended I wasn't excited to see him, that I didn't feel giddy, the beginnings of a schoolboy crush growing in my chest.

He grinned, and his easy charm shone through as always. "Getting you to break another one of your rules." Inwardly, I cringed. My first rule was not to see any alpha more than three times. They got attached that way. Unfortunately, I broke that rule with Guy a long time ago.

Another rule, somewhere down the line, was not to ever have them over to my condo. I didn't know how far down the line that rule was because since I'd implemented the rules, I hadn't made it that far down before. The first time Guy showed up outside my door, I sent him away with the same sort of flirtatious teasing, but as hard as it was, I held my ground. Now, not so much. Something about Guy had me throwing them all out the window lately, and the truth was, I didn't even care.

Guy held up a brown paper grocery bag. "Brought dinner. Wanted to make something special for a special omega." The eye contact was so intense I wanted to skip the food and go straight to bed. Guy sniffed the air, a cocky half-grin on his lips. "Seems like I have perfect timing."

"I can make meals for myself just fine, I'll have you to know."

"I wasn't just talking about the food, but if you can cook half as well as you do everything else," he lifted a suggestive eyebrow at me, "then you're a regular Wolfgang Puck."

I threw back my head and laughed. "Wolfgang Puck, huh?" "Obviously, you're way sexier than he is. C'mon, gorgeous, don't leave me out here in the cold." "The cold" was the richly decorated hallway of the expensive building I lived in.

I let out a long, exaggerated sigh. "We can't have you freezing to death, I suppose." I stepped back from the door and Guy strode in.

"Atta boy. C'mere." He caught me by the waist and swept me up into a kiss that made my head spin. When he let me go to make his way into the kitchen, I had to catch myself on my wobbly knees. Was this what I'd been wanting lately? It had to be. The perfect alpha was breaking down my walls, beating back all my defenses. I was being seduced by the slickest alpha around, and I loved it. That quiet voice in the back of my mind, though, it whispered to me. *This isn't right.* Again, I pretended it didn't exist.

Guy walked through my kitchen like he lived there, opening cabinets until he found my wine glasses and took two down with a gentle clink. Part of me bristled at the liberties he took in my house, but part of me liked his take-control attitude. He rattled through one of my drawers and pulled out the wine opener, setting a fancy bottle of red down on the counter with a soft thunk.

"Sit," he said. "Relax. I'm taking care of you tonight."

I slid into one of the tall chairs at my island, giving myself a front-row seat to watch this alpha- my alpha?- cook for me. "Ooh, I like that, big alpha."

Guy just smiled like he knew I did. He tipped my glass and poured me a generous share of an expensive Bordeaux imported from France. He pulled out a beautiful cut of meat wrapped in butcher paper and brown string.

"It's rack of lamb for you tonight. I'm pairing it with rose-mary red potatoes and asparagus."

"Sounds incredible."

"I knew it would." Guy turned to the sink, took one look at the mess inside, and burst out laughing. "We're gonna have to keep you out of the kitchen, I see."

"That's what I have you for," I quipped, trying to hide my embarrassment. I wasn't a fan of the way he laughed *at* me, not with me.

"That's right. You have me to cook for you now." Back to the gooey feelings. His words made it sounds like we had a future.

"What's the new hot goss in supply chain society?" I teased. Guy was in supply chain management of a fortune 500 company. I was successful, but what I earned was piddling compared to him.

"Things have been *interesting*, shall we say, with all the wild-fires going on."

"Is that right?" That was all Guy needed to go on for the next thirty minutes about how tight production had gotten and how difficult it was to transport things across the US-Canadian border, etc, etc. It was a lot of talking, but I admired his career. We saw eye-to-eye when it came to our work, and we considered ourselves equals, the best in our respective fields. Also, he was cooking me a delicious dinner after I burnt mine, so I wasn't about to stop his flow. I listened as he seasoned and prepped the lamb, got it in the oven, then cut and seasoned the potatoes and asparagus.

My need to talk about my job was ready to explode out of my chest when he said, "How's work going for you?" That got my blood pumping. Finally, I got to talk about my favorite subject. That was one thing I enjoyed talking about with Guy since we both were so passionate.

"It's phenomenal," I said, bouncing in my seat like one of the kids I operated on. "I've already performed more than a dozen surgeries this year and it's not even halfway through February. I think I can break my own record. Of course, I have to be careful not to stretch myself too thin or burn myself out, but I'm excited about all the families I get to help and places I get to see. My pocketbook isn't complaining, either."

"Wow, you're really going like gangbusters, huh?"

"Yes," I nodded enthusiastically as he drizzled a golden stream of olive oil on the asparagus, which was now perfectly cooked. "This is set to be my best year yet."

"Then you'll be out of town a lot?"

"I'll barely be home. I might as well rent this place out." I chuckled a bit at my attempt at a joke. Guy didn't look at me. He set the olive oil down on the counter with a little sigh and a small smile.

"I've been thinking, you know. About us."

I sat up straighter. "About us? You mean me and you, together?"

Guy leaned forward, resting his elbow on the island as he reached across and took my hand. All my hair stood up on end as I clutched his fingers, exhilarated by his touch, even though the back of my mind prickled, saying something was off. "I want to be with you. I want to take a stab at this thing."

"You do?"

"I do."

I gathered myself, remembering not to be too vulnerable. I gave him a little smirk. "What makes you think I'll agree to that?"

"I think you letting me in told me everything I need to know. It's symbolic, you know." Yes, I did know. "I think after you eat this dinner you'll agree to it. I think once I get you in the bedroom, you'll agree to it." I hated to admit it, but he was right. *This isn't right, though,* the little voice whispered. I shut it down, because I was about to get what I wanted. "Valentine's Day is coming up soon. Perfect timing for a romance, right?"

"Right," I said, even though I didn't really think so. Valentine's Day wasn't something I took seriously. "I'm gonna be out of town, though. I have surgeries to perform."

Guy rolled his eyes. "In Bumfuck, Minnesota."

"There are still kids who need lifesaving surgery in the midwestern boondocks."

"Right." He didn't sound convinced. "I wanted to talk to you about that, too. This is the perfect segway."

My blood pressure ticked up. "Talk to me about what?"

Guy came around the island, leaning on it in front of me. He rested his hands on my biceps and gave me a little squeeze. "Relationships require sacrifice, right?"

"Riiiiight," I replied slowly. *I don't like where this is going.*

"I don't want to have to spend special days without you. I want you close to home."

"Guy, I appreciate that, but my job requires that I travel. That's a major piece of it."

"I know, and I've been thinking about that. In order for us to be together, I think it would only be fair if you cut back on the travel."

He might as well have cut out my stomach. "Excuse me?"

"I know it's not ideal, but I don't think it's too much to ask."

"You don't think it's too much to ask?" I repeated, incredulously.

"Don't get upset. I can more than compensate for any reduction in your wages. I'm willing to do that just to spend more time with you. That's how much I value you. Value what we have, and what we could be."

I was shocked. "You wanting me to stop doing what I love is showing that you value me?"

Guy squeezed my arms again. "I didn't say *stop*, sweetheart. I said cut back. You can still do it for fun here and there. I just want you at home. What's so wrong with that?"

"My loss of satisfaction is what's wrong with that. My loss of independence is what's wrong with that."

"I just told you I'd take care of you. You won't want for anything. As a matter of fact, you'll live even better than you do now. I'll get you a nicer place than this." He lifted a finger and twirled it around, acting like the beautiful home I put my heart and soul into earning was a pigsty. My vision went red and my veins throbbed in my forehead. Who was this man I let into my home? I was only moments from blowing a gasket.

"You think this is about your money," I started, my voice dangerously low as I struggled to keep myself in check. "You think having a unique skill, that I went to college and studied fifteen years for and *perfected*, better than anyone in the nation," My voice got louder as my anger built, "that saves lives and that gives me a sense of pride and fulfillment, is worth throwing away for you."

Guy threw up his hands dismissively. "You're getting upset when I told you not to. There's no need to get worked up, Christopher, I'm not taking away from your skillset. It's one of the things I admire about you the most. I can't wait to show you off and brag to everyone what my omega can do."

"All while forbidding me to do it."

"'Forbid' is a strong word. I can't *make* you do anything, I can only ask you to make a few sacrifices for us."

The manipulation was outrageous. "What sacrifices are you going to make, exactly?" I snapped, not bothering to hold down my volume anymore.

"I just told you. I'll be taking care of the both of us. Especially if, in the future, we were to have babies. I really want babies, Chris. Can you imagine? A sweet little girl and a boy? I would think we'd want you home to raise them. You could take some time off, maybe even retire."

My eyes flew wide. "If you think I'm giving up my lifeblood to be your prize pig that you trot out for your little country club friends, you've got another thing coming. I'm not some pedestal for you to stand on while you chase your dreams and I abandon mine."

Guy laughed like I was a stupid, insolent child. "Listen. I could have gone with someone younger, someone more willing to please me-"

"You just called me old and washed up, and implied that you want a young, beautiful fool who has no ambitions other than propping up you and your ego."

Guy's face crumpled into something stormy, volatile. "I'm trying to give you something hundreds, thousands of omegas are begging me for. You're just throwing your chance down the drain because you're stubborn, egotistical, and selfish. I see why you're still single." Guy wasn't at all who I thought he was. *You knew better,* my subconscious said. The nerve of him to hurl insults that applied perfectly to him. Little did he know I could match him hurricane for hurricane. Things escalated into a shouting match as quickly as gasoline accelerated an engine fire.

I went to the door and yanked it open, pointing into the hallway. "Get out of my house and lose the directions. Don't ever contact me again."

Guy stepped just outside the door into the hallway. "You just lost out on Guy Guillaume."

I pretended to wipe the sweat off my forehead. "Thank god I dodged that bullet."

"You'll regret this, Christopher," he raged. "You'll never find another alpha like me. You, I can replace in the next ten minutes. Just you watch."

"I won't regret anything because I. Don't. Care." With that, I slammed the door in his face.

His muffled voice came through the heavy wood of my door. "You'll regret this, just you wait. You'll regret this!" His voice faded as he moved down the hallway.

I dropped back down at my dining room table, pretending his words didn't sting. Exhaustion tugged at my body, like someone had just turned up gravity. As soon as I was able to move a muscle, I'd drag my ass to bed.

Beep, beep, beep! My smoke alarm shrieked, jerking me back to life. Smoke was coming out of the oven.

"Motherfucker!" I ran over and grabbed my blue oven mitts, which were already seeing more action today than they had in the past few months when I first bought them. I yanked open the oven door and waved away the cloud of smoke that poured out, setting the red-hot pot on an eye of the stove. I waved at the smoke, trying to banish it out of the window to mingle with the rest of the Philadelphia pollution.

It took three tries with my broom to poke the little button on my smoke alarm that made it stop screaming. With any luck, the fire department wasn't on their way like last time. I'd gotten a couple of telephone numbers, but it had still been embarrassing the way a few of them condescended to me like I was a silly little omega who almost burned his own building to the ground.

"Fuck this." I picked up the bottle and took several healthy swigs, wiping my mouth with my sleeve when I was done. All the meat was overcooked and all the potatoes were under-cooked, but I shoveled a pile of everything onto a plate and took it back to the table along with the wine.

"Did I just go through a breakup? Can you even call that a breakup?" Whatever it was, it hurt like hell. I covered my face with my hand, humiliated. "I broke my rules for that asshole, thinking we were at the start of something, thinking we had a future. He treated me like such dirt. Like everything I worked for doesn't mean anything, only bragging rights for him while he made me worth less than him in our not-even-a-relationship relationship. What the fuck." I savaged the rack of lamb, snatching off a charred mouthful that crunched between my teeth, the acrid taste of carbon on my tongue. "Just wait until Jing hears about this." My best friend and frequent surgery partner had warned me about letting Guy get too close. I wish I had listened.

My phone buzzed over on the counter, the screen lighting up the dim, now-gloomy room. Maybe she was being psychic now and knew I needed her. She was good at that.

I snatched the phone up and answered it before looking at the screen. Big mistake.

"Oh my god, you'll never believe who just left."

"Who?" My O-Dad asked, in his gruff voice.

I laid my upper body across the counter, folding my forearms and dropping my head on them. "Hi, Papa. I didn't realize it was our time to talk." I dropped that hint because it *wasn't* our time to talk. He'd snuck one in on me.

As usual, he ignored me. "You said someone just left. Was it an alpha? Why'd you let them leave?" I banged my head on my forearm, glad he'd never gotten the hang of video calls so he couldn't see me beat my own head in.

"It was nobody important." That didn't stop it from hurting, or make me feel like any less of a fool. *You did the right thing,* said my subconscious voice. If letting a shitty alpha break down my walls and my rules, then having a major fight that ended in me alone was the right thing, what the hell was the wrong thing?

"Did you run another one off? This'll be, what, your thirty-fifth Valentine's Day single?"

I pinched the bridge of my nose. "Yes, yes it will." I hated Valentine's Day. I never cared about being single for that fake, commercialized holiday. The more time passed, the more I was determined to rebel against my O-Dad's pressure to be in a relationship. It seemed that whatever I wanted, he always shamed me for it and wanted the opposite for me. My best guess? It was a projection; whoever my alpha parent was, they were long gone before I was born. I carried a lot of shame around being an abandoned child, and my O-Dad was not one to let me forget it. He stayed single, sour, and negative, and no matter what I did, it was never good enough to get his approval.

I changed the subject fast. "It doesn't matter about any alpha. I'm heading out of town anyway."

"Where are you gallivanting off to this time?" He sneered.

It's not gallivanting, is what I wanted to say, but Papa wouldn't listen anyway.

I ticked the locations off on my fingers. "I'll be in Minnesota next-"

"Minneapolis? Rochester for the Mayo?"

"The Mayo's next. First, I'll spend a couple of weeks in Clearvale."

"Never heard of it."

"Me neither. The population is like, ten thousand. Not many people, but there are little lives to save, for sure."

"I just can't understand why you feel like you need to go

ripping and running all over creation doing your little surgeries."

He "didn't understand" because he wanted me close to home, where he could control me. How many times did I have to say this? "There's nothing little about these surgeries, Papa."

"That's not what I said."

"Yeah, it's-"

"Are you trying to tell me what I just said?"

It was moments like this that all my confidence went out the window, and I was that stupid, incompetent, unworthy kid all over again. I loved my father and he had his good points, but being an uplifting, supportive parent was not one of them.

"No, Papa. I didn't say anything."

"That's what I thought."

I became a doctor to impress him, to show him that I could make something of myself, that I could make big goals and whistle right on by them. Being the nation's leading pediatric heart surgeon at age thirty-five, which was practically unheard of, with a nice condo and plenty of money (which he had no problem asking me for) wasn't enough. Nothing was ever enough, but I was never able to get off the hamster wheel and stop trying.

He started up again, in that sour tone of his. "You know what I always say-"

"That while I'm worrying about everybody else's kids, my womb is drying up and I'll never have any of my own." I knew the whole spiel verbatim. I got it every third conversation I had with him. "I'm not in a rush to have kids. I tell you all the time how much I love my career. I may not have kids at all."

Papa blustered and blubbered on the other end of the line. I usually added that part just to rile him up. I did want a family, I did want to settle down. Just not right now, and nobody was gonna pressure me into giving up the impactful career I loved. Not my Negative Nancy father, and certainly not some alpha who wanted to control me.

While my dad went on a tangent about how I was focusing on the wrong things in life and being selfish and running around like a chicken with its head cut off, I imagined the perfect alpha for me. Would it be too much to ask for someone who *supported* my career instead of felt threatened by it? In my mind, someone gentle, shy, maybe a little inexperienced came to mind. Not likely. Those were the types of alphas you settled down with, but I liked the seductive fast-talkers, someone who could keep up. I shook the thought off. What would I do with a wholesome alpha besides eat them alive and break their heart?

"You're doing all these surgeries all the time," my O-Dad was griping when I brought my mind back into the excruciating conversation.

"It's my job, Papa."

"One of these days you're gonna make a mistake. Then what?"

"Okay, time for me to go." I hung up without another word. I gasped for breath. There was a tennis ball lodged in my throat and hot coals in my eyes. I swallowed it down and blinked them back. *I'm not gonna cry. I don't cry. I do need backup, though.* Now was the time to call Jing.

She answered on the second ring, her smile lighting up my screen. "What's going on?"

I laughed bitterly. "Could you smell my desperation and distress?"

"Coming off you in waves," she joked.

"Jing, what happens when I make a mistake?"

"We all make mistakes, Chris."

My voice came out small and I clutched at my smartphone, tiny in my hands. "With the surgeries."

"Shit. I need wine for this one. You do, too."

I looked down at my empty, trembling hand. "You're right. I had some, but I don't anymore. Why don't I have wine?"

The view on my screen jostled for a few moments as she poured herself a drink. "That's why I'm here. To remind you." She took a long slurp to punctuate her sentence. I relocated the bottle of Bordeaux, forgotten as I tried to manage the always-emotionally-damaging conversation with my dad.

"You settled?" Jing asked.

I took a sip from the bottle with my shaking hands. "Yup."

"What do you always tell me when I'm afraid of getting dosages wrong, or keeping someone under too long or not long enough?" Jing was an anesthesiologist, so she knew better than anyone about holding a life in her hands.

I took a deep breath and recited my words of support and advice to her. "I tell you that you're an expert at this. You're the best in the country, and I wouldn't work with you if you weren't. I wouldn't trust you if you weren't."

"What else?"

"That we've worked our asses off at this. We eat, sleep, and breathe it. Even routine surgeries can go wrong, but when they do, we know how to handle it and we've got each other's backs."

"That's right." She paused for a sip of wine. "We're a team. We hold each other up. The stakes couldn't be higher for us, but we do this because we can handle it. You got this. Take a deep breath and a big swig."

I took a shaky draught of my wine, swallowed, and filled my lungs with air. I let it out in a big sigh. "Thanks, Jing. You're a lifesaver."

"What happened? Talk to your dad?"

"How'd you guess?"

"I'm psychic."

"Then why didn't you call me before he did?" I whined. "That's not all of it. Guy was here right before I talked to Papa."

Jing rolled her eyes. "Here we go."

"I shouldn't have let him in."

"No, you shouldn't have. He also shouldn't have come to your place unannounced. The *entitlement*."

"I let him in, like an idiot. He brought me wine, cooked me dinner."

"This is gonna be a doozy."

"He said he came because he couldn't stop thinking about us. He told me…" I dropped onto my couch and let my head loll back against it, clutching the bottle to my chest with my free hand. "He told me he wanted us to be together."

"You told him hell-to-the-no like Whitney Houston, right?" I didn't say anything. "Right, Chris?"

"I didn't at first. Not until he started up about me making 'sacrifices' for us to be together."

Jing gasped. "No, he didn't."

"Oh, yes, he did."

"You kicked his ass to the curb, didn't you?"

"Right after I chewed him a new one."

Jing tilted her head, making an empathic face at me. "I'm sorry, honey. I always hoped you'd break your rules someday but that it would be for the right one, not the guy who threw it in your face, pun intended."

I tipped my head back on the couch again and pinched the bridge of my nose, stemming the tide of emotion. "There is no right one, Jing. Not for me. I don't want to be in love, I don't want to be committed. I'm happy with my life the way it is now. I don't want anybody else trying to control or change or shame me. Nobody else." I made a slicing motion with my hand, from left to right. "Nobody."

Jing nodded her head slowly. "Okay. I hear you. Maybe this next trip is just what you need. You can get out of Philly, get out of the city, clear your head, get focused on work again."

"If I could leave right now, I would."

"We'll be heading out before you know it. You never know, maybe there will even be a bumpkin alpha who will turn your head."

My subconscious perked up at that. It sounded right, but why, after what I just went through? I ignored it. "Not likely."

"You won't feel like this forever. I don't want an idiot like Guy Guillaume to be the reason you stop having fun and close yourself off."

"I'm done, Jing. At least for a while."

She held her hands out in front of her. "Alright, if you say so."

"I do say so, so don't go getting any bright ideas."

"Who, little old me? I would never." I gave her a playful stink eye. "Okay, maybe I've been known to get in some trouble here and there, but I'll keep my hands clean this time around. In the meantime, tell me about this new suturing technique you heard about." Grateful for the distraction, I launched into telling Jing all about it, trying to dull the ache in my heart. It lessened a bit, but didn't go away. *You'll be okay*, said the little voice. *It's coming. He's coming.*

What's coming? Who's coming? The way my heart rose, you would think there was some kind of miracle on the way. Maybe going to small-town Minnesota was just what I needed. I had no idea, in that moment, how my life was about to change.

2

TEDDY

Why, oh why, did I let my moms talk me into this date? I kept my eyes trained forward on the omega across the table from me, nodding along to what they were saying, but inwardly wishing I was anywhere else. Cooper was just…not my type.

"Excuse me. Excuse me." He snapped his fingers twice to get the server's attention. When they didn't respond fast enough, he stuck his fingers in his mouth and whistled, making everyone around us jump. "Ay, some help over here, please?" I cringed so hard. I was gonna die of embarrassment. Our server returned, with a "stiff upper lip for the sake of customer service" smile on their face, but they clearly wanted to throttle my date.

"How can I help you?" they asked.

"I'm not a fan of this broccoli, sir."

"I'm sorry to hear that. What's wrong with it?"

Cooper pointed at the menu, where there was a color picture of the meal. "Don't look the same. I thought I was getting this," he pointed at the picture, "but then you brought me this." He pointed at the food, which in all honesty, didn't look much different.

Our server put on their best smile, clearly practiced numerous times. "Let me grab our manager."

The manager was over in minutes and my date reveled in the attention, suppressing a grin in favor of looking hacked off. Maybe it gave him a sense of power to be able to order someone else around.

"This food doesn't look like the picture. I want what I ordered."

The manager was clearly much more practiced in "the customer is always right-isms," and was able to look much more sincere when she said, "We can't have an unsatisfied customer, now can we? I can comp that for you."

"Comp?" Cooper asked suspiciously.

"That means there will be no charge."

"Oh. You could just say that, you know." I looked skyward, wishing help would drop out of the ceiling. *Please, let me drop dead right now.*

The manager tilted her head and smiled. "You're right, I should have been more clear. Would you like us to make you another there, hun? Or something else?"

"No, don't go to all that trouble. I'll just make do."

"Are you sure? We'd be happy to get you something else."

He turned his nose in the air, surprisingly dramatic for someone wearing flannel. "No, no, this'll do just fine."

"Okay, sounds great. You both let me know if I can help you with anything else tonight, okay?"

"You bet," I choked out. I gave the manager my best apology smile, and gave another one to our server, who was across the room watching the whole exchange with a scowl. *Thank god I'm not in Clearvale.* Both of our towns were so small, there was no way either of us would be able to get away with that kind of behavior without everybody, down to our second grade teachers, knowing about it.

Cooper shuffled in his seat, settling his elbows on the table next to his plate. "There. Now I get it for free. Almost as good as bagging a ten-point buck."

"Mm-hmm," I said, even though I was *not* a fan of shooting things. Cooper was like most folks around our neck of the woods; he liked to hunt, fish, snowmobile in the winter, four-wheel in the summer. I didn't get into it in the same way. I wasn't rugged or outdoorsy, definitely not enough to keep up with him. "I was going to pay for it."

"Thanks, but now you don't have to worry about it." He looked around, his lip curled up in a sneer. "I can't stand places like this."

I looked around. It was a nice restaurant with modern decor and a grayscale color palette. "Places like what?"

"These fancy places where people act like they're better than you."

My brow furrowed as I tried to think of what he might be talking about. "I don't think anyone's acting like that here."

"Oh yes, they are. They know when you don't frequent these kinds of places and they treat you different." Oh. He was insecure because he was a rube. There was nothing wrong with that. I was the definition of a rube, and so was everybody I knew. Sometimes we felt a little out of place, but we tried not to make it everybody else's problem.

I dug into my meal, a parmesan-crusted salmon, but it didn't taste very good to me because I wasn't enjoying the company the way I hoped I would. "Our server is nice," I tried. "He seems really attentive and like he wants you to enjoy your meal."

"No, he doesn't. He's judging me, so screw him. I can't

imagine what the people who own this place are like. I just got a freebie off them, anyway." Jeepers creepers. We needed a change of subject, immediately.

"You were telling me your folks got a new combine."

"Sure did. The one they had kept kickin' for thirty-two years with a little maintenance here and there."

I grinned, resting my elbow in the table and my chin in my hand. "They don't make 'em like they used to, do they?"

"Sure don't. Sugar beets for you, right?"

"Yup. That was my grandparents' lifeblood, on both sides. That's how my moms met."

"That's sweet. In all senses of the word." Cooper smiled, and I mirrored his smile. For the first time I felt a connection, like maybe we were getting somewhere. My body responded, too. Just a little flicker of arousal and the thought that, *maybe*.

"Soybeans in your family, right?" Cooper crossed his arms and sat back in his seat, a fond, faraway look in his eyes as he reminisced. It gave me the chance to look at him. He was nice to look at, for sure. Fit and strong, in the way a lot of farm kids were.

"Soybeans and a little corn mixed in, some hogs, too. Feeder pigs."

I nodded along. "Nice. I bet you pulled some long hours, helping out your folks."

"Like you wouldn't believe. I'm glad for it, though. Makes you tough, teaches you the meaning of hard work, you know?"

My attraction to him grew a little stronger and I thought, *what if?* "For sure."

"I loved running in those cornfields. Getting lost, blocking out the rest of the world. It was special."

"Yeah, sounds like." I breathed a sigh of relief. Things were going so well now that we'd gotten through the rocky parts. *I think we're really warming to each other.* I leaned forward a little, not realizing just how warm Cooper was.

He lowered his voice and dropped his chin. "I disappeared into those cornfields for a lot of things. I wasn't always alone."

I furrowed my brow, clueless as always. "You mean you went with brothers and sisters or something?"

Cooper had a good laugh at that one. "No, not like that. I mean, we'd go play, for sure. I'm talking about a different kind of playing. The kind alphas and omegas get up to." He bounced his eyebrows at me. I shrank back a little without meaning to. *Ho boy, I think he's flirting.* That was the part where I always got confused and screwed things up. It never failed.

"Oh, well," I let out a nervous laugh. "Playing lots of tag?"

He tilted his head back and forth and gave me what was clearly a suggestive look. If I was catching on, that meant he was being *super* obvious about it. "Of a kind."

I dropped my eyes to the remains of my salmon, sitting abandoned on my plate. This was going into unfamiliar, uncomfortable territory, as my dates often did.

"That…sounds like fun, too, I guess." I wouldn't know, but I sure as hell wasn't gonna tell him that.

"It was. Maybe I can show you sometime."

I rubbed at the back of my neck, getting red and hot under my fingers. "You mean, like, play tag? I wouldn't last long. I'm clumsy as hell, got two left feet."

"I'm sure you'd *last* longer than you think." I walked right into that one, didn't I? The problem was, I had no idea. I hoped, when the time finally came for me to *be* with someone for the first time, that I lasted long enough to please them. I just didn't know. It was embarrassing enough having never even been kissed at my age, but to be a first-time minute-man on top of that? All of Clearvale would hear about it in less than twenty-four hours, but I'd have died of embarrassment already, dropped dead on the spot.

"Um…" I fidgeted in my seat, nervous and overwhelmed and intimidated. I didn't know what to say, so I said nothing and an awkward silence hung between us for a second. Cooper was persistent, though.

"That's all there was to do, sometimes. Disappear into the corn fields, play a little game. You know what I'm saying?"

I cleared my throat. I remembered those days, when everybody else was doing it and I was just standing around, blushing and waiting for somebody to pick me, and when they didn't, hightailing it home to hide and lick my wounds.

"I remember those days," was the most I could come up with.

"Did you sneak off to a lot of cornfields?" He asked, a salacious grin on his face.

"Oh, I snuck off, alright." I didn't like the turn this date took. I was somewhere between turned on by Cooper's body and the good parts of our conversation, turned off by the not so good parts, and scared half to death because he was experienced and pushing for something sexual, and I wanted to be ready, but I just didn't think I was. I looked around, trying to find some sort of life preserver to get off this sinking ship.

"I gotta say, Teddy, I think you're a really good-looking alpha. You look like you know how to handle a snowblower." He laughed at his joke, but the suggestiveness was still there. I perked up a bit at him thinking I was good-looking. It made me wonder if I was making a mistake. How many more chances did I have left?

"Yup, gotta make sure my moms' driveway is cleared," I tried. It was a horrible joke and I sounded like the total lame I was.

"You're funny," he said, and it was his turn to lean forward. "I'm a really direct omega."

I took a swig of my drink, desperate to help my dry, scratchy throat. "I noticed."

"I'm interested in you. Sexually."

My voice came out squeaky. "Oh, yeah?" I took another shaky gulp of my drink, sloshing a bit of it on my chin. I wiped it off quickly. *Classy, Teddy.*

"Yeah. So I wanna know. What kind of sex do you like? What do you get into?" He was coming on to me hard, and the prospect of finally getting *it* over with and having sex for the first time was thrilling…but did I want it to happen like this? Cooper was okay, but did I really want my first time to be with him? It wouldn't be special. Was it stupid for me to want it to be special?

"Oh, I, uh, I guess I like, uh…" I yanked at my collar and hoped there wasn't visible steam coming out, I was so terrified. "I guess I like it when it's slow and sweet. When there's a connection, you know? Maybe even love."

Cooper stared at me for a second, eyebrows raised. Then he burst out laughing, slapping the table with his palm. "Oh, that's good!" The smile dropped off his face as he saw my grimace paired with my blush. "You're serious. You really want the Hallmark movie, 'look deep into my eyes while we make sweet, sweet love' experience?"

I shrugged, keeping my focus on my plate, not daring to see how he must be looking at me. "I mean, why not? Isn't it better when you feel something?"

Cooper went right back to laughing. "That is so tenth grade. If I didn't know any better, I'd think *you* were a virgin."

I looked up then. "I'm not." I lied with an edge to my voice, then dropped my eyes back to my much-less-intimidating cutlery. "Even if for some strange reason I was, what's wrong with that?"

"Everything's wrong with that, it's a huge red flag. You're what, twenty-seven?"

I bristled. "Twenty-eight. Why a red flag?"

"Nobody stays a virgin until they're twenty-eight."

"It's not impossible," I mumbled.

"It's pretty damn close."

I rubbed a hand over my mouth. "I beg to differ," I muttered.

"Listen, I can see this virginity stuff is making you a little riled up, and not in a good way. We don't have to keep talking about it if you don't want to. We can go back to what we were talking about before."

I relaxed a little. "Thank you, that sounds great." What I didn't realize was that by "before" he still meant the subject of sex.

Just then, something touched my shin. I realized too late that it was Cooper, trying to make contact in a suggestive way. Before my brain puzzled it out, it had already panicked and sent a message to my leg to respond by kicking. A literal knee-jerk response.

My foot connected with Cooper's shin.

"Ow!" Cooper jerked back in surprise and yelped in pain. He cursed, reaching under the table to massage his shin bone.

"Oh, no," I whispered. I just took things from bad to worse.

Cooper slid to the end of the booth, pulling his jeans up to look at his leg for damage. Thankfully, there was nothing big or obvious, but had I kicked him hard enough to bruise? Absolutely.

"Oh my god, I'm so sorry. I didn't mean to do that, I swear."

"I was just trying to play a little footsie," he said with a pained smile. "Guess I took it too far."

"No, You didn't, it wasn't…I just reacted before I knew what was happening."

"Gotta be honest, here, Teddy. You don't seem like you're into it."

"No, it's not that, it's just…" That I'm a virgin and I'm intimidated? Cooper waited. I didn't have a good answer. There was more awkward silence, and it was even worse than before. Whatever this date was, it was over and I knew it. The worst part was, Cooper was giving me a pity smile. *Anything but the pity smile.*

"Y'know, it's getting late and I'm kinda tired."

"Yeah," I said, unable to look at him anymore. It was only seven o'clock in the evening. "I'll grab our server and get the check." I scuttled off to find them and hand them my credit card, anything to expedite the process and get away from the embarrassment of yet another failed date.

After I paid and Cooper got the doggie bag he insisted on for his "hard-earned" meal, we walked out of the front entrance. I didn't know what was colder, the weather or the rock in the pit of my stomach.

"Welp," he rocked from his heels to his toes, hands in his pockets, keys jingling as he touched them. "We tried, right?"

I dropped my head, glaring at the ground. "We tried." I failed. Hard.

He fished the keys out and twirled them around his fingers, looking at out at the parking lot like it held the answers to all his prayers. "I'll keep in touch."

"Great," I croaked. "Sounds great."

He gave me an awkward handshake, holding himself a yard away from me, then practically ran off into the dark.

I beat a hasty retreat to my own vehicle, so at least I had a private place to burn in the fires of humiliation. I dropped my head onto my steering wheel, which gave up a half-hearted honk.

"They should bottle up my essence and sell it as omega repellent," I muttered, my mouth and nose full of leather. "What the hell happened tonight, Teddy? What's wrong with you?" Where to start? Was it that Cooper and I weren't compatible, or did I not try hard enough? Was I just too damn awkward to seal the deal with an omega, even when they were practically throwing themselves at me?

I admired anyone who knew what they wanted, but omegas who were direct like that were overwhelming. They were sexy and cool and sure and I was just too inexperienced to handle someone like that. It didn't matter, because I couldn't go through meeting any omega ever again.

The engine whined as I turned the key in the ignition, sputtering a bit from the cold before turning over and roaring to life. Cold air blasted from the vents. It would be a few minutes before the engine heated up enough to blow warm air in.

Just as I was about to pull off and get away from this hellhole, my phone vibrated, lighting up in my pocket. I groaned, knowing exactly who it was. I answered without looking. My alpha mom. "Hey, Ma."

"Hey, son." Her tone was excited, anticipatory. From the echoing, tinny sound of her voice, it was clear she was on speaker phone. "I'm here with your Mama. Tell us how it went!"

I balled up a fist and put it up against my forehead. I hated to disappoint them yet again. "It was bad."

"It was bad?" Mama's voice came in, and it had that sinking, "you poor baby" sound to it. It was both comforting and grating at the same time.

"Matter of fact, it was horrible."

"You're kidding," Ma said.

Mama's voice was distressed. "But, but…from what Janice told me, you and her son were the perfect match."

"He was cool in a lot of ways, but did she tell you her son was insecure and kinda rude to waitstaff?"

"That's no good," Mama said.

"Nope. It's not that we didn't have some good spots, or that he wasn't attractive." I squeezed my eyes closed for a second, thinking about how I dropped the ball on possibly banishing this stupid virginity once and for all. "He was not the one for me." That might have been true, but I didn't do myself any favors by kicking him when he made a move on me. There were a few seconds of silence on the other end. *Here it comes.*

Mama started in first, her voice full of pity. "Oh, honey, it's perfectly okay. That omega didn't deserve you."

"Yeah," Ma added, she was enthusiastic, but it was underlaid with disappointment. "Plenty more fish in the sea. You just gotta keep *putting your bait* out there."

I groaned. "That never sounds right, Ma." They said the same thing every time, and every time, I believed it less and less. My moms were supportive, loving people, but they were constantly setting me up on dates, and constantly disappointed when I inevitably struck out, or when my date was a dud, or both, like the double whammy of tonight.

They knew I'd never had sex, had never even been kissed, because I was an only child and had been telling them everything since I was old enough to talk.

"Sweetheart, don't get discouraged, okay? When the time is right for you, it'll all fall into place. You'll find just the right person for all your firsts."

I tightened my hands around the steering wheel, making the leather crack under my palms. "Mama, please. I don't wanna talk about dates anymore. I don't wanna go *on* dates anymore. I need a break."

"Don't say that, Teddy. If you give up now, things will carry on like this for who knows how long?" Translation? Give up and you'll stay a virgin forever. They meant well, but they put so much pressure on me. Then, when things didn't go according to plan, their pity made me feel so ashamed.

"Something has to be wrong with me, for there to be no omega within a one-hundred mile radius who wants to kiss me."

"Are you kiddin'?" Ma said. "You're our son, which means you're a handsome, hardworking gentlealpha."

"Thanks, Ma." I knew she meant it when she said that. I was hard-working, I most certainly minded my manners the way they taught me because I was a good Minnesota boy, and well, I'd just have to take their word for it on the handsome thing, because I wasn't sure if I saw it.

"Oh, that's a good idea, too," Mama said.

"What is?"

"The hundred-mile-radius thing. Maybe we should be looking outstate for you. Maybe we can fly somebody in." She was joking, but I knew she would totally try it if I okayed it.

"Mama, please. I don't want my hopeless love life to be opened to a nationwide search. Just local omegas rejecting me, please."

"There must be something we haven't thought of," Mama said.

Ma jumped in. "I can ask around at the shop, see if anybody knows a single omega or beta around your age."

"Or maybe even not around your age."

I sighed and held my hand up to the vent. The engine was

heating up now, and warm air tickled my palm. "Ma, you've already asked around at the shop. A couple of times."

"Wouldn't hurt to do it again. You never know what might have changed. Maybe somebody's fresh off a divorce or widowed."

"Okay, okay, I think it's time for me to go."

"We're sorry, honey. Things will get better, okay?"

I tried for a wan smile. "Yeah, I know. Thank you for trying to help. I love you both."

"Love you, too," they both chorused in unison.

"Bye." We clicked off, and as I drove home, I let myself fall apart.

I desperately wanted someone special. What did it feel like to be in love? To be caught up in a tornado of passion toward someone? To kiss a pair of soft, pillowy lips? To be overtaken by lust and make love all night long?

What about making a family? Would I ever get the chance to have little ones?

"I'll never know," I said out loud, my voice barely audible over the rush of heat from the vents. "Never. Never ever. If it hasn't happened now, it's not gonna." In the back of my mind, some small part of me begged to differ. I wanted to be hopeful, wanted so bad to tune in and listen, but I was tired. I was burnt out on keeping my dream alive. It was easier, safer, to just let it go now. *Don't give up yet,* it said. *Leave me alone,* I said back. *I'm tired of hoping when I've got no hope left.*

Closed in and safe at home, I bent over the bathroom sink, rubbing the tears from my eyes. The shame stung like a swarm of bees, surrounding me in a buzzing, angry cloud. Why did I have to be like this? To believe that love conquered all, and that sex should be special? Was I that naive, to believe in those things when the world was so fast-moving and unfeeling and cutthroat? I had to be wrong, because at twenty-eight, here I was. I needed a miracle, but I wasn't getting one.

I looked at myself in the mirror. My eyes were bleary and red. My cheeks were stained with tears, which embarrassed me even more. I wished a hole would open up under me and swallow me into it. If not for my moms, I'd find a spaceship to get on and fly away into the galaxy, never to be seen again.

"Beam me up, Scotty," I muttered, scrubbing at my face too hard, making the skin raw and painful. "One damn thing's for sure, I'll never go on a date again. I'll die an un-kissed, unloved virgin."

Little did I know that the next day would send me hurtling toward my true destiny, a collision course with the omega of my dreams.

3

TEDDY

"You're our last resort, Teddy. Tim dropped out because he has a stomach flu. We *need* you to be in the auction." Dr. Gupta leaned forward on the counter at the bustling nurses' station. Around us, bed wheels squeaked as patients were transported through the eggshell-painted halls. Nurses chatted with each other, some pointing to digital charts on iPads. The sterile hospital smell burned the inside of my nose a bit, but I was so accustomed to it I no longer smelled it.

I was shaking in my boots but tried hard not to show it. I surreptitiously grabbed the counter and squeezed, holding on for dear life while a friend and colleague that I looked up to tried to convince me to do what felt like trotting myself out at a meat market. Or like being a lamb sent to slaughter. "Me, get up on a stage and get auctioned off with candy like I'm, well, candy? I can't do that, Dr. Gupta." Especially not after last night.

Dr. Gupta chuckled. He held his hands out in front of him, palms up. "What are you so afraid of, Teddy, that all the omegas will rush the stage to attack a handsome, single alpha like you?"

I gulped. I literally could not imagine that scenario. No omegas were rushing me. "Handsome?" I echoed, fussing with an iPad, my fingertip making a *tap, tap, tap* on the surface.

"Don't you have a mirror at home?"

"Yeah?" I was still confused. I looked at myself every day and saw a pretty regular guy, short blond hair, brown eyes, tallish, nothing special. As much as I wanted an omega to see me as special, it hadn't happened and some days I wasn't sure it was ever going to. I'd spent every other Valentine's Day alone; I didn't see this one being any different.

"Earth to Teddy?" Dr. Gupta waved a hand in front of my face. "There you are," he said as I snapped back. "You really have nothing to lose, besides an evening at home. The hospital needs the money. You know how badly we want to expand our omega and baby wing."

I grimaced. I did know. They were doing such great work over there, working to give omegas a peaceful, comfortable delivery in which they felt supported and listened to. They were making it a point to offer equal care to omegas of color too, knowing that Black omega parents especially died in childbirth at an alarming rate, with a whopping sixty percent of the deaths preventable.

"Do it for the babies," Dr. Gupta said, gently prodding my shoulder.

"For the babies," I ground out.

"Good man!" Dr. Gupta gave my arm a little punch this time. "You never know. You can go right home if nobody picks you, but it's impossible no one will want a date with a fine young man like you, especially on Valentine's Day."

I lifted my eyebrows. I respected Dr. Gupta's opinion, so this meant a lot. "You think so?"

"I know so. As a matter of fact, you just might find your

dream omega. Maybe they'll pick you right out and you can live happily ever after." My heart clenched in my chest. Wishful thinking. It would be wonderful, but in reality it was impossible and I was still determined not to give in to *hope*. There was nothing I wanted more than my very own omega to love and a family to care for. I wanted a baby as badly as I wanted to breathe, and to finally spend a Valentine's Day with someone to love, treasure, and cherish? It would be a miracle. *Too bad virgins don't make babies. Who wants a virgin my age, anyway? They'd think I was some kind of freak.*

Dr. Gupta continued, "There are some wonderful professionals in from out of town, as well. For example, Dr. Chalmers."

Information about the medical virtuoso circled all around the hospital, and all of it was either high praise or speculation about his relationship status. "The one who's performing Delores' heart surgery."

"Exactly. Maybe he'll be there."

My smile was wan. An omega like Dr. Chalmers picking me? I couldn't see it. "I don't know about all that, Doctor. I promise you this, though. I'll be a good soldier and fall in line for the babies."

"Yes. Fall in line right up on that stage, and get yourself chosen for this special holiday. Fall in love once you leave it." His smile seemed to say, *I know how badly you want this. I believe you can have it. I believe in you.*

The faith and encouragement was all a little too much for my heart to handle, so I took my leave. "Gotta go make the rounds. See you soon."

Dr. Gupta held up a finger as I walked away. "Tell me how it goes!" He called after me. "I want an invite to the wedding!"

I chuckled, shaking my head as I headed down the hall,

dodging heart monitors and phlebotomy carts. "If your well-wishes get me hitched, Doc, I'll give you a front row seat."

I rapped on the door of room number 212, where my favorite patient, Delores, was awaiting heart surgery. I started my 7 AM shift soon, right before the sun rose, but since I was here early and they'd come for her shortly, I decided to stop by and give her a sort of a send-off.

"Come in," said a kindly but haggard voice. It was Delores' mother, Rhonda. She smiled at me as I walked in, but it didn't reach her eyes. The bags were dark smudges against her skin.

"Nurse Teddy Bear!" The four-year-old girl, Delores who was named for her grandmother, had a hard time sitting up in bed. She even had a hard time speaking loudly, and it broke my heart to see it every time. My only consolation was that I was helping her get better. That expert surgeon who came in from out of town, Dr. Chalmers, would do the hard job, though; the part that would save her and alter her life for the better. I might never meet him, but he had my respect. I'd like to shake his hand just once, though. *Just because he's excellent at what he does and he's saving an adorable child. Not because I'm curious and think it could go somewhere.* At least, that's what I told myself.

I grinned and crouched next to the bed. "How's my favorite patient today?"

"I'm great! I'd be even better if I got my hug." She held her arms out for me. Her parents chuckled at her sweet brassiness while I practically fell over from how cute she was, honored by her affection.

"Oh, well, excuse me." I sat down on the bed so I could give Delores' tiny, frail body a big hug. She was sick and weak, but she sure didn't hug like it. I crushed her up against my chest, enjoying the joy of her innocence and love, along with the softness of her little afro puffs tickling my cheek. I needed her to be alright, for my own sanity.

"Oh, my goodness, you're so strong." I pretended to gasp for breath from the strength of the hug as Delores laughed triumphantly. "What a warrior! You're gonna kick this surgery in the teeth."

Delores got quiet at that. Somber. "Will you be here when I wake up?"

I'd be off work and getting some rest before my next shift, then preparing to get auctioned off tomorrow. Maybe to Dr. Chalmers? *Don't be silly, Teddy.* "When you first wake up, your momma and daddy are gonna be here."

She waved a dismissive hand at me. "I *know* they'll be here, they're my momma and daddy. What about you?"

I suppressed a smile. "You'll still be very sleepy when your surgery is over. You'll sleep tonight, like usual. In the morning when you wake up, I'll be right here." I would be right back at work, so I could check on her and keep my mind off the auction and possible upcoming Valentine's Day date. *Not* with Dr. Chalmers.

"Okay." She chewed on her lower lip.

"What's the matter, honey, are you scared?" She nodded, her eyes as big as saucers. "Don't be. You got the best doctor coming in to help you. You're gonna be good as new when this is all done. Better."

Delores' dad, James, cleared his throat. "You know, Teddy, we heard Dr. Chalmers is not only talented, but single and quite a looker."

My face turned into a furnace, and I immediately started blubbering. "I, well, I, uh. Heard some things. Good things. Not the single part, though." *Good job, Teddy. That was graceful.*

Rhonda waved a hand at her mate, laughing. "Don't pay him

headed to my favorite specialty confectioner's shop. I stomped the snow off my boots when I entered, the shop's aesthetic glowing golden and warm in contrast to the winter weather outside. The special was milk chocolate truffles with a honey center. I'd never heard of that before, but it sounded intriguing and delicious. I imagined the omega that chose me would have a full mouth with red-bitten lips. He'd take a bite of the chocolate and the honey would spill out and drip down his lips, golden and sticky. Yeah.

It's a good thing I don't know what Dr. Chalmers looks like so I can't insert him into my fantasy. Or is it?

I headed home to shower and change into a pair of black slacks with a crisply-pressed green button-down. I shaved and put on a bit of the cologne my sister insisted on buying me "so I could smell as good as I looked."

"I clean up pretty nice, I think," I said to my reflection in my foggy bathroom mirror. I wiped a palm down the surface with a *screech*, leaving a clear stripe in the condensation to get a better look at myself. "Yeah, not bad."

There was no one there to offer their opinion one way or another. Maybe tonight all that would change. Maybe, if nothing else, Dr. Chalmers would be there for me to meet him. He didn't have to bid on me. He didn't need to go on a date with me, or fall in love with me, or any of that. I could just tell him thank you.

Off I went to the charity cattle drive. I didn't really want to get auctioned off. Maybe no one would pick me and I'd get to go home. Truthfully, deep down inside, it would break my heart if I didn't get picked, or if someone bid on me and my honeyed chocolates because they pitied me.

Maybe, my heart said with a little lilt, *Dr. Gupta will be right* and your perfect omega will find you. Maybe it'll even be that handsome Dr. Chalmers, like Delores' parents said.

Impossible. My brain protested, while my heart whispered, *Miracles happen every day. Nothing's impossible.*

Little did I know, as I ran a finger across my collar, nervous and overheated as I prepared to go on display, the chocolates shaking in my trembling hands, the impossible was right around the corner.

4

———

CHRIS

"Is it gonna hurt?" The four-year-old in an Avengers hospital robe asked me. Her brown eyes were big and mournful, full of tears. Her chin was tucked against her chest, and her head was leaned into her mother's bosom, flattening one of her cute little afro puffs, lined with gold from the light of the chilly but beautiful sunrise.

I was in the Chance Vieth Children's Center of the Willow Green hospital in Clearvale, Minnesota, where I'd traveled to perform several surgeries. I was crouched down in front of the girl, Delores ("named after my grandma!" she proudly told me), in her bright, colorful hospital room, but we were taking her into surgery soon. Cold air, stainless steel, blue scrubs.

The nurses and techs scurried around us, getting everything prepped. In the surgery suite they were laying out equipment, making sure the room was sterilized, gathering everything needed to perform an intensive, life-saving surgery on a tiny, vulnerable little body. I looked up to her mother, whose lip quivered as she pulled her baby a little closer, held her a little tighter.

I gave Delores' arm a gentle poke with a fingertip, which brought a small smile to her face. "Nope. We're gonna have you put on a cool mask-"

Her face brightened up. "Like Bane?"

I grabbed that and ran with it, since it helped her not to be afraid. "Yeah, like Bane! Even makes the cool hissing noise, too. It has special air in it that'll help you sleep like a baby."

She crossed her arms, her little brow furrowing. "I'm not a baby."

I chuckled. "I know, honey. You'll only sleep like one. Your mom and dad will be right here waiting for you. Me and my friends are gonna fix you right up, and when you wake up you'll be right back here."

"But it's gonna hurt after?"

I winced. "I'm afraid it's gonna hurt later, yes. Once you get all healed up, though, you'll be able to run and jump and play."

"Play soccer and basketball?"

"Yup. Since you're a big girl, I know you can be brave."

She pulled her sleeve back and flexed her skinny little arm, tiny muscles flexing under her brown skin. Her big eyes got serious again. "You promise I'm gonna wake up?"

I blinked. What a question from a girl who'd seen way too much in her short little life. I'd done the procedure dozens of times before. I was the leading performer of this form of pediatric heart surgery in the nation, but there was always a huge risk and I didn't make any promises I wasn't sure I could keep.

I rested a gentle, reassuring hand on her thin knee. "I'll be with you the whole time. I'm the best in all of America at what I do. I go all over the country doing these surgeries and it's my favorite thing, helping big girls like you get better. So I plan to help you get better. Okay?"

She gave me a serious nod. "Then you and nurse Teddy can bring me your baby."

This weird thrum went through my entire body, like I was a harp and someone just plucked my string. "Excuse me?"

Delores gave me an adorably exasperated look. "We decided that you and Teddy are gonna have a baby and bring them back so I can meet them."

I was confused. Delores must be talking about a plushie or something. I certainly couldn't make a baby with a stuffed bear. I was never the type to believe in Valentine's Day. Sometimes, when I was in a new town, an alpha would catch my eye and we'd have fun for a few days until I did my work and it was time for me to leave. I never wanted to stop working long enough to look for a mate and have babies, but taking the stuffed animal part of out it, for some reason this sounded *right*.

"Who's Teddy, honey?" I asked. Maybe if I got more clues, it would all make sense and explain the rushing feeling of *yes*.

Delores' mom jumped in. "Don't worry about that, Dr. Chalmers. She's just repeating something she *thought* she heard earlier."

Delores put her hands on her hips, waggling her head. "Mo-om, I know what I'm talking about. I want that baby." My strings kept vibrating, faster and faster, creating some sort of beautiful music in the back of my psyche that I strained to hear.

"What did she hear earlier?" I asked. Unfortunately, I never got my answer.

"Doctor? Are we ready?" Right behind me stood a nurse with his equipment, ready to administer the beginnings of the anesthesia.

I turned back to Delores, shoving the thrumming down for

now. I needed to focus. "Ready to turn into Bane and get this party started?"

"Yeah!" I held up my hand and she gave me a strong high-five, making the room echo with the slap.

I shook my hand out, pretending it hurt. "Wow! You're so strong. This surgery is no match for you."

Delores' parents lifted her onto the rolling bed and laid her down. The nurse's confused face was hilarious as Delores did a happy wiggle, reaching out to pull the gas mask over her face, eager for them to strap it on.

"Thank goodness she loves Batman," her dad said, stroking her arm as the nurse gave her instructions.

"Delores, I want you to count backward from ten for me," the nurse said. "Can you do that?"

Delores looked affronted. "Yeah, I can do that!" She inhaled and the machine hissed. "Daddy, I really sound like Bane!" She shouted, the sound muffled by the mask, the fog from her breath clouding the plastic.

"That's great, baby. Start counting like the nice nurse asked you to."

"Okay. Ten. Nine. Eight..." Delores' eyes drifted shut.

"Showtime," I mumbled to myself, slipping into Surgery Mind. I turned to her parents before my "transformation" was complete and I became more robot than human. "I know how precious she is. I'm gonna take damn good care of her."

Delores' mother ducked her head, hiding the tears. Her father simply rested a hand on my arm, nodded, and squeezed. *Go save our baby,* his eyes said. I intended to do just that.

Not long after leaving Delores' hospital room, I found myself in full blue surgical scrubs in front of a stainless steel sink, water falling from the faucet and drumming into the massive basin as I scrubbed my arms down with antibacterial soap. The lather was thick and white against the dark hair on my arms, the smell sharp and sterile. After rinsing my hands I held them straight up, elbows bent. My staff slid on my plastic gloves. After that, I was in full Surgery Mind.

I was nearly dissociated as I approached the table with the sea of blue surgical drapes with a square of brown skin exposed; an impossibly small torso. Delores.

For the moment, I forgot about the special little person underneath and focused only on the scalpel in my hand and every precise cut I needed to make. Jing was right there as my anesthesiologist. She gave me a solemn but encouraging nod. *You got this.* My blood hummed with the thrill of doing what I was most passionate about in the world, the thing I dedicated every waking hour to, to the point I had no life outside hospital walls. What else could I possibly need?

A stealthy whisper in the back of my mind said something I couldn't quite hear. The word "love" seemed to float around back there, but I shoved it down. I wasn't ready to be in love, and besides, I had more important things to focus on.

I held my hand out. "Scalpel."

I made the first cut.

Twelve hours later, with the final stitches closed in Delores' little chest, I snapped out of Surgery Mind back into the room, to the soft applause of my team. I breathed deep, grounding myself in the here and now once again.

I nodded to the group of people who came together to save a life today. "Thank you. Thanks, everybody. Couldn't have done it without you." I gave Delores' arm a final rub. Jing would reverse her anesthesia and get her safely back to her room with her parents soon. Exhausted, I dragged my ass out of there, stripping out of my surgical scrubs as I went.

I had just enough energy to pop into the waiting room

where Delores' loving parents sat huddled together, looking for all the world like they were outside shivering in the cold. Their eyes held a million questions for me, but I answered the first one straight away.

I smiled. "Delores did great. She was a real star." They collapsed against each other with long sighs as I crouched down in front of them. "Everything went off without a hitch. They're reversing her anesthesia so she'll be in recovery for a while, but after that you can see her." The couple couldn't have been happier. They squeezed me in hugs that smelled like Dior perfume and mesquite woodsmoke.

"Miracles are gonna happen for you, Dr. Chalmers," Rhonda said. "Just you watch." *You and Teddy are gonna bring me your baby.* The words from the innocent four-year-old plucked at my heartstrings, but why? She was talking about a stuffed animal and not a human, right? Even if she was talking about a human, I had no idea who it was. I'd never meet them, and there's no way they'd be the one for me anyway, not enough to make a whole other person with them. *Why are you thinking so hard about this, Chris? You're not looking for love anyway. You're one of those cliche married-to-your-job types.* I snapped myself out of it.

Rhonda and James held each other tight, finding relief in each other's embrace. It might be nice, to have someone like that through thick and thin.

"You need sleep, honey," I murmured to myself as I half-walked, half-drifted to the on-call room. After a while, Jing appeared in the dim light of the quiet little space, sitting up with her head tipped back against the wall and her eyes closed. She opened them slightly to look at me.

Her voice was soft and sleepy. "Another successful surgery, Doctor Chalmers."

"Couldn't have done it without you, Doctor Li." I sat next to her and wrapped an arm around her shoulder, giving her a little squeeze.

"Uber's on its way."

One less thing to think about when my body and brain were already on empty. "Have I told you how much I love you lately?"

"I can always stand to hear it again."

"I love you."

"Love you, too." Jing let her eyes flutter closed again. "You know, we deserve something nice after this. We deserve to *celebrate*. I know this is our profession and we love to do it, but we should give ourselves a little more credit for a job well done." Her phone blinked, illuminating the dim room. "Ride's here."

We leaned on each other as we walked to the entrance of the hospital, the sliding doors whispering apart to let us out into the cold night air. We strode to our ride fast; for some reason, we both kept forgetting we needed to bring our coats with us here.

"I wouldn't mind celebrating, especially after saving Delores. She's such a special kid. What did you have in mind? You can never go wrong with a little champagne."

She twisted her hand with a flourish as she climbed into the backseat of our ride. "Champagne will *always* be involved. I thought we could go to a nice, upscale dinner. Something where we can mix and mingle. It'll even be for a good cause."

I leaned against the window of the black SUV, half-asleep until I heard the uptick in the tone of her voice. I cracked one eye open to squint at her. "Sounds like a trap already."

"It's not a trap," she said, with her signature nervous laugh that bubbled up anytime she had a trick up her sleeve.

I was fully alert now. "Woman, what are you trying to drag me into?"

The ride was already over since we were staying only

minutes from the hospital. The SUV pulled smoothly into the driveway of our cute, classy AirBnb, a nicely remodeled bungalow with four bedrooms, three bathrooms, and all the amenities traveling physicians could dream of.

"I heard about this event while we were at the hospital. It's a Valentine's Day auction," Jing said, right before hopping out of the SUV, slamming the door and making a break for the house.

"What do you mean, a Valentine's day auction?" My raised voice echoed into the night, my breath coming out as a white, ghostly mist that floated up into the night. She had my undivided attention now. I hopped out and followed her to the house, where she pointedly didn't look at me as she dug out the key and twisted it in the lock.

"It's a lovely event where you go and bid on candy and get a surprise date." The keys jingled as she got the door unlocked and rushed inside, trying to get distance between us because she knew she'd be in big trouble for volunteering me for a date. I wasn't a fan of Valentine's Day and Jing knew that. That wasn't even taking into account the little matter of what happened with Guy just days ago.

"A surprise date?" I exclaimed behind her. She power-walked away, trying to get to the kitchen, but I grabbed her and playfully tackled her onto the plush floral loveseat. To be honest, it felt really nice after coming in from the cold. "You're making me go on a date, lady? When you know I don't do that? When you know what happened with that alpha clown who I let in my condo?"

"To be fair, I'm making myself go on one, too!"

"How is that fair?"

"Because I sprang for the tickets!"

"You what? You little sneak, you already planned for us to go to this auction behind my back? You know that even without what happened with Guy, I'm not a fan of that schmoopy Hallmark crap." The words came out of my mouth, yet somehow this time they didn't feel totally accurate. There was a tiny part of me that thought, maybe. Miracles. Teddy bear babies. *Snap out of it, Chris.*

"I *know* you're not a fan, that's why I did it behind your back."

I pretended to throttle her on the couch, gently shaking her shoulders. "No more emotional crap, Jing! I refuse!"

"Come on, Chris, it'll be fun. When's the last time you went on a real date, and not one with a dick barging into your condo? I know you're a sexy, rich, surgeon omega and you get yourself laid all the time, but when's the last time you felt a real connection?"

"Who says I'm gonna feel a connection now? Who says I *wanna* feel a connection now?" *Maybe...*

"Who says you won't and don't? I know you took a risk with Guy, but you knew he was flying some red flags."

"Don't remind me."

"You can't know when you'll find a *good* alpha, the *right* alpha, until you take a risk, and you love surprises."

"That's true, but..." *Why am I resisting so hard? What do I have to lose, really? Just my career, my home, and my sanity. In all seriousness though, I'd gone through the worst of it already. What if I meet a teddy bear and bring Miss Delores her baby? Jeez, when did I lose my mind?*

Jing's brow wrinkled into her dead-serious, laser-focused, heading-into-surgery face. "It's to raise money for the children's wing. The omega and baby program."

That made me sag like somebody cut my strings. "Ugh. Hit me right in the heart, why don't you."

Jing took advantage of it and made her escape to the other side of the couch. "Don't mind if I do."

"Fine, I'll go, but on top of helping a good cause, I better have a good time."

"I know you, Chris, you'll have a good time. Besides, anything could happen. I feel a miracle coming on."

The strange but pleasant, honey-sweet thrumming filled my body once again. "Everybody keeps saying that."

"Then it's gotta be true. We've all gotta be geniuses."

"Go to bed, genius." I smacked a kiss on her forehead.

She stood up from the couch and walked toward her room, stumbling a little as the fatigue took over again. "Get plenty of rest so we'll look our best for all the hot alphas tomorrow."

"Oh my god." I rolled my eyes, but I was smiling. "Night, lifesaver."

"Back at you."

As I moved my bumbling feet toward my own room, I reflected on how I'd given another precious child their life back today. It was a gift to have the ability to do that. I was forever grateful, but what if there were other pieces I wanted, that would fit into place just right, but I hadn't made room for them? I banged my shoulder on the doorframe in my sleepiness and distracted state. I'd give it more thought tomorrow. Right now, I needed sleep.

I didn't bother to change my clothes. I dropped facedown onto the downy sheets, the mattress catching me in a supportive hug. I lost consciousness almost immediately, but before I did, thoughts of "you and Teddy bring me your baby" and "miracles are gonna happen for you, Dr. Chalmers" danced in my mind. My heartstrings thrummed one last time. Then, I was dead to the world.

"How did I even end up here?" I muttered, tugging at the

lapels of my turquoise dinner jacket, trying again and again to rearrange them, lay them perfectly flat, anything. Jing swatted my hand. It was the next evening and she had somehow finagled me into a nice suit and dragged me out of the house to a fancy hotel, where the fundraising event was in full swing. We were still being idiots and forgoing our coats for our vanity, so I shivered a little. As much as I was fighting it, I wouldn't mind an alpha to warm me up, Maybe I'd find the right one for the job tonight. Just for one night, though. The date, and I promised myself that was it.

Jing halted me inside the soaring atrium, just inside the main entrance. She straightened my matching tie and smoothed down my lapels. "You ended up here because you're a workaholic with commitment issues. Also, you can be a grump."

"Bah humbug."

She gave my tie a gentle tug before deeming me suitable for the auction. "What if you happen to buy the love of your life? Take the key and drive a brand-new alpha right off the lot?"

I offered her my arm and she looped hers through. I patted her hand reassuringly. "With my luck he'll be another one that's certified pre-owned with a ton of baggage in his trunk."

"Nothing wrong with a little baggage in the trunk." Jing twisted her hips for emphasis.

"Of course not. We love the junk in the trunk. We don't love the emotional baggage."

The music, soft conversation, and clinking of champagne glasses swelled as we approached the main event. A brass band played in the grand ballroom of the hotel. Dozens of people, dressed in formal wear in rich colors and the finest materials, milled around with glasses of wine and tiny white plates with hors d'oeuvres. They smelled like designer fragrances and lots of money.

Jing whistled. "They really laid out the red carpet."

"Gotta get the omegas and babies lots of dough."

She squeezed my arm. "Gotta get us some dates."

I thought back to my conversation with Delores. "With our Teddy bears?" I asked with a chuckle.

Jing's brow scrunched. "What?"

"Huh?" *You're talking crazy, Doc Chalmers.* "Nothing, I didn't say anything." Jing gave me a look, but didn't ask any questions.

We made our entrance, stopping in the arching hand-carved entryway, her in a burgundy evening gown with a slit that was just this side of decent, me with my dinner jacket, my hair parted and combed, and black slacks that showed off my assets. If there were any alphas looking my way tonight, they'd get an eyeful. Something to pull them in, make them want to make miracles with me. No, I didn't mean that. That sounded like emotional attachment. They could make sweet music with me. One night only.

Jing tugged my arm, bringing me back to reality. "Let's go find our alphas."

First we found our table, a round eight-top with a gold, embroidered tablecloth, gold chargers under delicate white soup bowls, and gold silverware.

Jing plucked a small blush tea rose from the bouquet and tucked it in my lapel. "There. Now we're ready."

The candies sat on individual white pedestals near the stage, their boxes on display with little lamps illuminating them in soft light, warm in tones but not temperature.

I strolled up to the first display in the row, scanning over it with my eyes. "Oh, I see how it works. The bachelors list what they've planned for the date and the candy they picked, and we roll the dice depending on what they're offering."

Jing leaned forward a little to read a date card next to a box of assorted fancy chocolates. "I don't think it's as much of a roll of the dice as you think. The kind of date says a lot about them, what they like to do, and what they think is putting their best foot forward. The candy tells you, well, whether they have decent taste buds."

I snorted as I stepped to the next display. "Cherry cordials and a trip to the county fair? Cute, but not for me." I moved on to the next display. "Roasted almond toffee chocolates and dinner at the opera house. Fancy. Maybe a little too fancy."

The next box caught my eye. There were already prospective bidders milling around it and I wanted to budge past them, tell them to move along because this show was over.

I approached the display cautiously, eyes fixated. The box was a shimmering gold wrapped with a red ribbon. The prospective date was with an alpha, a trip to the local wildlife preserve. Blood rushed to my ears. That had never been my jam before, but for some reason, I wanted to try it. This alpha cared about nature and loved the great outdoors. They must be sweet and down-to-earth, literally. Nothing like Guy at all. The problem was, the salt-of-the-earth types usually couldn't handle me. I was a little too bold for them, a little too modern. *This time, it'll be different. Maybe.* That thrumming feeling was back, a gentle pluck of a single string inside me, but it made my whole body vibrate and dream of miracles.

The deal was sealed when I got a load of the kind of candy I'd be bidding on. Milk chocolate truffles with a honey center.

"A honey center?" Jing said, coming up alongside me. "I've never heard of chocolate with a honey center before."

"Me neither," I mumbled, my eyes glued to the decadent sweets before me.

Jing nudged my shoulder with her own, the soft fabrics of our garments rubbing together. "Sounds sexy."

"I know." When I bit into it, would the chocolate shell be crisp and melt in my mouth, and the honey blend in for that extra touch of luxurious sweetness? I imagined honey dripping down my lips, and suddenly I was a little moist.

"I'm bidding on this one," I announced.

Jing scrambled for a pen and handed it to me. "Do it."

I wrote my name and a number with a healthy amount of zeroes behind it, feeling a rush like I'd never felt before. "That ought to do it. Tasty chocolates, help for the babies, and a date to a nature preserve with a sweet alpha who might be super sexy, too. Let's hope I'm not making another huge mistake."

Jing beamed. "You're doing the right thing. I knew you had it in you."

A couple of glasses of champagne, a rousing speech, and a petit sirloin later, and it was time to announce the winners of the auction. I sat up straighter in my chair, surprised by how much I wanted to hear my name announced as a winner. Honey truffles and a wildlife refuge. This alpha had me so curious I couldn't sit still.

The MC went right on down the list, naming the winners of the cherry cordials and the fancy almond chocolates, showing off the bachelors behind the candy under the bright lights of the stage.

Jing elbowed me. "They're easy on the eyes. Ours better be, too."

I bounced my heel up and down on the floor like a mad seamstress. "If we win."

"We're gonna win," she whispered, just as the MC turned to the box of honey truffles.

"Now, ladies and gentlemen, we've got our unique offering of milk chocolates with a honey center. I've never heard of that before. Have you, Jim?" He asked the assistant just off stage. Jim shrugged and shook his head, a cheerful smile on his face. The MC continued. "The date is to our lovely local wildlife preserve. It's another unique offering and a beautiful, peaceful one out in nature. Let's bring out our one-of-a-kind alpha to go with it. I happen to know this guy, and the winner is in for a, well, a treat, pun intended." A few more of my strings were thrumming now. I squeezed my hands into tight fists, fingernails biting into my palms. Who is he? The one I'd visit Delores with, carrying a new baby? I shook out my shoulders and refocused on the stage, applause reaching my ears just as a man stepped out of the darkness and on to the stage.

My lips fell open and my jaw hung slack. He was the most perfect alpha I'd ever seen. The alpha put his hands in his pockets, tucking his chin and hunching his shoulders.

Jing put her hands on my shoulders and shook me. "He's all yours!" She gushed.

"We don't know that yet," I managed, my mouth dry and my eyes trained to the stage, drinking my alpha in. At least, I wanted him to be my alpha. *Not forever, of course,* I lied to myself, *but for the date.* Then again, the way he looked, he had me thinking about forever.

Jing hung off my shoulder, hissing in my ear. "I don't know why he's so nervous, look how hot he is. He *should* be in front of everybody. On display. Preferably without clothes."

"Hey, don't talk about my date that way. He's one of those shy guys." Wallflower alphas weren't typically my jam, but in this case I'd gladly make an exception. "I love it. More of him for me."

"Glad you bid on him, aren't you?"

"Glad I'm gonna win." I didn't tell her how much I bid on my shy guy, but it was most certainly going to be helpful to the kids.

The MC held the mic up to his mouth and spoke, his voice filling the ballroom. "Congratulations to Dr. Chris Chalmers, your bid is the winner-" he stopped, his eyes popping out of his head as he looked at the amount on the card. He leaned over to Jim. "Is this right?"

"Sure is."

He turned the corners of his lips down in a "Well, I'll be darned" expression. "Chris, your winning bid has bought you a date with the one and only Theo Behrens!" Jing shrieked and clapped her hands hard. I just sat there. Did I get struck by lightning?

Theo Behrens, alpha from my wildest fantasies, lifted his head, his sweet brown eyes wide as he looked back and forth, looking just as shocked as I felt. Was he surprised someone picked him?

The lightning had charged me up, and I was ready to meet this guy. I stood up from my chair and the spotlight fell on me. I just grinned at him, waiting for him to see me.

When Theo finally caught my eye, his widened even more. His face paled and he visibly gulped. He held up a hand and gave me a small wave.

Oh, this is gonna be so much fun. I blew him a kiss. He blushed a bashful tomato red and tucked his chin again, a big ridiculous smile on his face, and what a smile it was.

"I might be a little in love with him already."

Jing nudged my shoulder. "See? You bought yourself an alpha tonight, fresh off the lot. That one looks like he has zero mileage."

I tsked at her. "Now, Jing. We both know better than to use crass metaphors to describe alphas. They're human beings. And I definitely want to take that human being out for a test drive. I wanna be the first driver behind his wheel, if you know what I mean."

"Oh, I know what you mean. Just don't eat him alive, okay?" Theo made his way off the stage on shaky legs and shuffled toward us with small steps, his chin tucked, his hands in his pockets, still fully blushing. He looked like he wanted to come closer but he also wanted to run, and that made me want to chase him. Tackle him. Devour him like the predator I was.

I winked at Jing. "No promises."

5

———

CHRIS

THEO HELD HIS HAND OUT TO ME, TRIPPING OVER HIS FEET A little. "Dr. Chalmers. You're the real, actual Dr. Chalmers."

I took his hand, heavy and wide with thick fingers. Workman's hands, inherited from people who worked the land from sunup to sundown. Fingers I'd like to have in my mouth. The truth was, while I was having plenty of physical thoughts about Theo, my emotions were strangely high. They shouldn't be. I wasn't breaking my rules ever again. I shook it off, but I didn't let go of his hand.

"You know who I am? Has word gotten around about my troublemaking already?" Apparently, I'd jumped into full-force-flirt mode. It made Theo blush, and damned if Theo's blush wasn't my new favorite thing.

His voice squeaked a little on the way out. "Yes, I...no, I mean, I've heard so many great things. It's an honor to meet you."

"So the slander hasn't reached you yet. Call me Chris, okay?"

Theo dropped his chin, grinning hard. "Okay, um, Chris. I

mean it. Everybody's been talking about how you swoop in and save the day, giving so many kids their lives back. It's really something special."

There was that damn strumming at my strings again, like Theo Behrens was plucking them himself, right now, with those thick, strong fingers. I was touched, right down to the recesses of my heart. He was so open, so pure with his admiration, like the spotlight from moments ago had never left me. Add that to the list of feelings I'd never felt before.

I squeezed his hand a little tighter. "Thank you, Theo. You flatter me."

"Please, call me Teddy."

For a moment, I just blinked at him. Could lightning strike twice? "Call you *what?*"

"Shhhh!" Jing said beside me as applause went up. Oh, yeah, there was still a whole auction going on around us. "Sit down, okay? You got your new model, now let me get mine!"

I bit my tongue in order to quiet down. Teddy and I sat at the same time, in one fluid motion. He took the now-empty chair right next to me, our knees practically bumping together. For a shy guy, his presence was so strong. Even when I turned my head to focus on the stage, there was still this hyper-awareness of where he was in space. The close proximity was unnerving, but in the best way. Everything felt so good; what was the catch?

A little signal went off in my brain and I noticed something, a point of connection. I dropped my eyes. My hand was still joined with Teddy's. He was focused on the stage like a good pupil in his favorite class. He didn't realize we were still holding hands either, until he saw me looking from the corner of his eye. He did a double take when he saw our hands still linked, then looked at me in a panic. He tried to pull his hand away, but

I wouldn't let him. I was wearing a full-on smile, and not even my seductive one. The corners of my eyes were soft as I watched his expression change back to bashful, blushing and grinning. He reminded me of Flower from the kid's movie Bambi. He turned his face against his shoulder, hiding from me but squeezing my hand a little tighter. *I think this one's special, Dr. Chalmers,* came the secret voice in the back of my mind. *One worth keeping around, seeing if a few miracles happen. Correction, I'm not keeping anyone around,* I thought to myself, *I'm just enjoying the thrill of something new, having fun with him while I'm here.*

The MC announced a different alpha, bringing them up on stage.

Jing slapped my arm hard enough for it to hurt. "That one's mine!" I didn't even feel it because all I could do was stare at Teddy. *I want you and Teddy to bring me your baby.* What are the odds?

"Our generous winner is Jing Li."

"Hell, yes." Jing jumped to her feet. "Bring mama the honey!" She leaned down next to me right before she took off. "Maybe that's your line, with your special chocolates and special alpha."

I fixed Teddy with a stare that was sexual, appraising in nature. I couldn't help it. He brought it out of me. I was used to being seduced, used to a game of wits and banter, but not this time.

As it turned out, someone had brought the chocolates over and set them on our table when I was wrapped up in both Teddy and the auction.

"Oh," he said, startling a little at seeing them on the elaborately decorated table. "Guess I forgot those when I came offstage. I was just really eager to meet you."

Wow. This guy didn't play anything close to the vest. It was all out there, heart on his sleeve. Should I unpin it, tuck it into my chest pocket over my own heart, secure it there for safe keeping? It was his genuine nature that had me fooled. *Gotta be careful not to get drawn in with this one.*

I leaned over and beckoned Teddy closer, whispering in his ear. "Those chocolates are so unique. I'd never heard of them before, and I just had to satisfy my curiosity, you know?" Teddy just nodded, his head bobbing up and down fast. "May I try one?" His head bobbed up and down even faster, and it was so damn cute and innocent.

I plucked a chocolate from the box, round and plump with honey, lovely chocolate lines drizzled on top for even more visual aesthetic. I held Teddy's eyes as I pressed the treat between my lips, savoring how the smooth chocolate melted on my tongue. My default with alphas I was attracted to was to add a little sex appeal, but I had it turned all the way up today. I was more than attracted to this man, I was already smitten. All that lust and unexpected emotion rolled into one made me a force to be reckoned with.

I bit into the chocolate with a soft, satisfying *click* as I crushed the shell between my teeth. Honey rushed into my mouth. A tiny bit dribbled down my lip and Teddy audibly gulped, his Adam's apple bouncing like a bobber on the surface of a lake.

I chewed thoughtfully and licked my lower lip, loving how Teddy's wide eyes tracked the movement. "This combination of flavors is surprising, but they come together really well. It's so sweet my veins are pumping pure sugar water. I can't get enough." At this point, was I talking about the chocolate or the man? Somewhere along the line, my brain whispered a single word; *mine.*

We didn't notice the event was coming to an end until they

brought the house lights up. Both of us startled out of our trance as the room flooded with brightness, assaulting our eyes and reminding us we were in a room full of dozens of people, not our own little world. We tuned back in to the emcee.

"We'd like to thank each and every one of you for coming tonight," he said, his face a beacon of hope. "Thanks to your generosity and sense of adventure, we've raised a *substantial* sum for our omegas and babies. We still have donations coming in, so keep a close eye on your email inboxes so we can tell you the final amount and the steps we'll take within the program using the money.

"For the winners of the auction," he bounced his eyebrows, his expression sly, "we can't wait to hear all the stories you'll have to tell about your dates. If we here at Chance Vieth are lucky, we'll hear about a new mated pair, and maybe even some little ones we helped create. Guess what? You can deliver them right here in safety and comfort, thanks to the expansion of the program. We can't wait for that day."

When I chanced a glance at Teddy, he was already looking at me, eyes as big, soft, and bright as twin moons. When I caught him, he cut his eyes, pretending he wasn't just staring at me like I was the Mona Lisa. Would it be too forward to tell him that I liked it? That I bathed in his attention? That he could look his fill because I was his and he was *mine?*

Get ahold of yourself, Chris. The date hasn't even happened yet, and once it's done that'll be it. "Should we go somewhere a little more…private? Discuss the details?"

Teddy looked almost troubled. "Of the date?"

I had to tease him, I just *had* to. "No, the plans for the new stoplight on the edge of town." Now he *really* looked confused. "Just kidding. Yes, I meant the date."

"Oh!" He lit right back up, popping out of his chair with a

spring in his step. "Yes, please, let's do that." He held out a hand to help me up, like a true gentlealpha, and once again, I took it. Once again, I held on.

I cast my eyes around the huge room, looking for Jing. I didn't want to just leave her hanging because that wasn't what bffs did. A big hand-wave toward the middle of the room caught my eye. A sea of people walked by, obscuring my view every few seconds, but it was plain to see Jing was wrapped up in an alpha man with a body like a model. Jing gave me an exaggerated wink and a thumbs up toward Teddy. She'd be alright, and she was encouraging me to go "be alright," too.

We held hands all the way out into the hallway. Once there, Teddy and I leaned against the wall, our shoulders against the antique velvet wallpaper as the last stragglers left the party and the space around us became quiet, still. The scent of gourmet food and fancy fragrances still hung in the air, but there was something else, too. Teddy's scent. It was sweet, as sweet as the honey in his chocolates. He'd put on a nice cologne, but his true scent shone right through. I moved a little closer to get a bigger whiff of the scent. Our fingers still played against each other, teasing, shy, exploring.

I watched him intently as he stumbled over his words, trying to stare at my face but avoiding my eyes. "I thought w-we could meet at th-three, get an early start, you know?"

"Three? I thought we were having dinner after."

"We are. It's just, there's a lot to see. There's so much I want to show you. The quaking bog, the animal rehabilitation center, the woodlands..." His nervousness disappeared as he talked about the wildlife center. Yes, that's what I hoped for. To see the man in his element. We were so close to each other we could kiss, and it wasn't out of the picture for me. I was known to take an alpha to bed the first night if they really turned me on, and Teddy the Shy Guy was on a whole new level.

"It sounds awesome."

"You think so?" Teddy asked, his brown eyes big and hopeful. He grimaced and rubbed at the back of his neck. "I wasn't sure. I thought maybe it might be too corny or too nerdy or, you know. Just lame."

I *did* know, because I hated to admit that's what I would have thought before. Now, with didn't-know-he-was-hot Teddy Behrens in front of me, even a quaking bog sounded like a great time.

"I think it's a reflection of you, and that's what important. I picked the date because it sounded interesting. I picked you." That brought the grin back to his face and boy did it make my heart drop down to my toes. "Bring on the bog."

We got all the details squared away with the meeting spot, what to wear, and directions- Teddy gave me a little printout of a map that had the route and the entrance highlighted. His thoughtfulness was such a pleasant surprise from what I was used to, what I expected, what I put out myself.

When we were done, he kicked at the ground in an "aww, shucks" kind of way. "Okay, guess I should let you go then, huh?"

I pulled out my phone and tapped away with my thumb to request an Uber. "Five minutes away."

"Walk you to the door?"

Hmm, that was strange. I didn't feel like Teddy was being too eager or too clingy, which was how I normally felt in these situations. No, right now, I wanted to hang on to this alpha as long as possible. *No, you don't. You're a player, and you just tried to turn your card in last week and look what happened.*

"I'd love that. C'mon." I jerked my head toward the door.

Teddy's hand found my lower back, ushering me ahead of him like a true gentlealpha. "After you."

I let myself enjoy it. Just for the moment. "Thanks, Teddy."

Outside on the curb we stood next to each other, not saying much but still vibing together. His button-down was green, a great color on him. The sleeves were now rolled up to the elbow like he was ready to do some farm work at a moment's notice, the muscles in his forearms corded and veined. The body under that shirt must be something else. I raised my eyes to his, taking him in as the hotel's entrance lights shining from behind gave him something of a halo. *I want you*, I said with my eyes. *I have to have you.*

Just as I was about to take a step forward and do something stupid, my Uber pulled up, barely making a sound besides a few pebbles crunching under the tires.

"Ope, I think that's you." Teddy held his hand out like we were ending a business meeting. "It was great meeting ya. Looking forward to Valentine's Day."

I held back a little laugh, looking down at his hand. He was so innocent, he hadn't caught on to my eye-foreplay from a moment ago. I bypassed his outstretched hand, swerving around it and coming in close, wrapping my arms around his back. The way he returned my hug was fierce. He was passionate and intense under all that Minnesota-boy wholesomeness. *I'll bring it out of you, just you wait.*

The Uber driver tapped on his horn, just a quick little *beep*, and we finally broke apart. I pressed a soft, lingering kiss on Teddy's cheek. His lips parted in surprise and he literally put his hand to the spot my lips just touched. *How can I handle a man so earnest? Goddamn, he's gonna be the death of me.* I didn't just climb, I was *lifted* into the backseat of the SUV by the lightness in my spirit, just from being around my alpha. *Don't do that, Chris.*

Don't let this accidentally-charming prairie boy make you think about the "L" word.

Teddy closed the truck door for me. "Have a good one. See you Valentine's Day, right?"

"You can bet on it." I blew him a kiss as the truck pulled off. He stood for a long time, just watching me ride away in the truck. I snuck one last look at him, too, nice and stealthy because the windows were tinted. Just before the truck turned the corner, I saw Teddy pump his fist in celebration. I faced forward and threw my back against the seat, both my hands over my heart. It pounded like a piston in my chest.

"He's *definitely* gonna be the death of me," I murmured, both a smile and the memory of his stubbly cheek on my lips.

The driver grinned at me through the rearview mirror. "Successful night with your special guy, I take it?"

I closed my eyes and let my head drop back on the seat. "My friend, you don't know the half." If I didn't watch out, Teddy would slip right under my skin.

An hour later I was buzzing around the house in my blue silk pajamas, nursing a glass of red, when Jing walked in. Her hair and clothes were rumpled, and she had a big smile on her face. "Looks like we both had good nights."

"Get lucky with your alpha?"

"Just a little makeout session. Frisky, but saving something for the honeymoon." She winked at me as she walked further into the living room, kicking off her sparkly Jimmy Choo pumps. She was being sarcastic, of course. I couldn't make those kinds of jokes about my date right now because I would, unfortunately, take them seriously. "Get lucky with your alpha?"

"Sure did," I muttered, not looking up from the extra wine I was pouring in the kitchen, "I gave him one whole kiss on the cheek."

Jing gave me a sideways look. "Who are you and what have you done with Chris? I thought you wanted to jump his bones, not be all sweet on him."

"I did!" I waved the bottle around, a sign of all my pent-up nervous energy. "I tried! At least, I tried to try."

Jing pointed at the bottle, motioning for me to pour her a glass, too. "Don't make me quote Yoda." I pouted as I tipped the bottle of red into a second glass, watching the rich liquid slowly fill the bottom half of it. She beckoned me over.

I set the wine on the coffee table and dropped down on the couch next to her with a huff. "I don't know what to do, Jing. He's got me so confused and I've only known him for like five hours."

"Confused? How? He seems like a straightforward kind of guy. The most straightforward guy who ever lived."

I threw my arms up and let them flap down in my lap. "That's the problem. I'm used to alphas who have game. They know that we're only in it for fun. We go on the hunt, we seduce each other, have a good time, and we get back to our lives. This guy…He stares at me so openly. It's obvious that he really thinks I'm somebody special."

Jing looped an arm around my shoulder. "I got news for you, babe. You are."

"I know, I mean…Don't get me wrong. I like myself. I'm proud of myself. It's just that Teddy has this honesty about him. This, like, purity. I don't know, it's like he floated down to me on angel's wings."

Jing took a swallow of her wine. "Jesus, you *do* have it bad."

"Don't tease me, lady, I'm having a crisis."

Jing shrugged a shoulder, teasing me anyway. "Doesn't sound like a crisis to me."

"It *is* a crisis, Jing! He acts like me kissing him on the cheek is some sort of…"

"Miracle?"

"Yeah." I didn't want to use that word, but there seemed to be a common theme here. *I'm in deep shit.* "What do I doooooo?" I moaned, throwing myself down on the couch with all the drama of a Broadway actor. I rested my head on her knee and covered my face with a pillow.

Jing snatched it off and gave me a gentle bop with it. "I'll tell you what you do. Absolutely nothing."

"Nothing?"

"Nope. It's time to stop resisting. Forget Guy, he can go to hell. I told you this might be your time for love, and maybe, just maybe, it is. If you're ever gonna find out, you have to stop trying to control it. Let the wave take you." She pointed at me with the same hand she held the wine in. "You float down this damn river of love, Dr. Chalmers, and see where it leads. Maybe it leads somewhere special. Some unexpected place that's so beautiful you can't even imagine it. Like, a loved-up, sexy oasis or something."

I sat up quickly before my imagination ran away with me. This feeling was too big to hold in my skin and I was fit to burst. "Rivers don't have waves," was all I could think to say. "That's the ocean."

Jing wasn't impressed by my attempts at sass. "Yeah, whatever. It was an awesome analogy and you know it."

"I do," I groaned, burying my face in her shoulder.

"Just let the river waves take you, Dr. Chalmers." He could hear the smile in Jing's voice as she lifted her arms and made flowing up-and-down movements with her hands, jostling my head on her shoulder.

"Let the river waves take me. I can do that. I think. I hope. I can find out where they go." Could it be to a loved-up, sexy oasis? Did I dare to dream it this early in the game? Would there be any babies involved?

On Valentine's Day, a day I had scorned all my life, I was about to find out.

6

TEDDY

I FIDGETED WITH MY FINGERS, STANDING ON THE SIDEWALK outside the main entrance to the Wildlife Center's visitor center. The wind picked up a little and I hunched my shoulders up toward my ears, but that was partially out of nervousness. My eyes scanned back and forth, looking out over the prairie and over to the woods, waiting.

I shifted from one leg to the other as my thoughts careened back and forth, batting each other across the court like a game of tennis.

"You gave him the right directions, Teddy. But what if I didn't? You did. But what if he doesn't show? He will."

I looked up at the overcast sky as if it would give me answers. I still couldn't wrap my mind around it all. Out of all the people who could have come to the auction, who could have bid on me, who could have *won*, it was Dr. Chris Chalmers, the super-suave surgeon who saved my little Delores. If the family knew, they'd freak out.

"*I'm* freaking out," I mumbled. I stopped pacing and shoved my hands into my pockets. I took a deep breath through my nose. Smelled like snow. We might get some later, but we hadn't gotten much this winter and it was unseasonably warm, which was why I felt like we could pull off an hour or so outside, as long as we kept moving. "He's gonna have fun on this date. But is he, though? Yes, because you did a great job of planning, and you're gonna treat him like the king he is, and you're not gonna mess up your shot. This won't be anything like that last date."

A black SUV rounded the corner into the long drive, and it looked like the same truck that had taken Chris home last night. I wanted to crap myself I was so nervous. *Play it cool, Teddy.* Yeah, right. I'd never been cool a day in my life.

The truck stopped next to the curb with a slight hiss of its brakes. Out stepped a vision. Chris wore a navy down hooded coat that somehow fit him like a glove and showed how broad his shoulders were. How his body looked so good through a bunch of layers, I had no idea. A wisp of his dark hair snuck out from under his gray beanie. He smiled at me in that intense way that he had. The way that made me want to hide because his sheer presence was so big, but pinned me in place and had me begging him to devour me all the same.

Can't think like that, Teddy. Shouldn't assume. Assume what? If Chris found out I was a virgin, he'd probably laugh at me just like Cooper did. An omega like him could have and would have had anyone he wanted. He would know what he was doing. The thought made me sweat despite the cold weather. As Chris approached me, my mind slipped in a few dirty thoughts. What if he didn't mind I was a virgin? What if he wanted to teach me? I shouldn't get my hopes up again. Should I?

I jerked myself out of my trance to greet my date. It wouldn't do to be rude, now would it? "Chris. I'm so glad you came." He had no idea how glad.

"Did you think I wasn't gonna show?"

I gulped as he stepped up to the curb. What should I do? Would going in for a hug be too forward? I loved the last one so much. I stuck with my manners and held out my hand for a shake.

"I didn't know for sure. I hoped so."

"Well, I wouldn't have missed it." He smiled at my outstretched hand, clearly amused. "I think we're past hand-shakes now, don't you?"

"Are we?" I practically wagged my tail like a puppy dog. Chris put his arms around my waist and I put mine around his shoulders, pulling him in close and tight. I tucked my face in his neck, nosing at the soft skin there, scenting him the way his alpha would. *Careful with the alpha caveman behavior, Teddy.* Chris didn't seem to mind. He squeezed me tighter.

I closed my eyes and held on. A lot of affection and the slightest hint of lust bloomed in my body. This already couldn't be more different than my last sorry excuse for a date. My lips were against Chris' neck when I murmured, "Can't believe I get to hold you like this." He shivered, just a little bit. Uh oh. I pulled back from the hug then. "You're cold. Let's get you inside." I put an arm around his back and guided him to the door.

He chuckled. "I'm not cold."

"Yes, you are," I scolded. Keeping Chris safe and healthy was now my top priority, the way it should be if you were a good alpha. "You're shivering, I can feel it." For some reason, that made him laugh harder. I didn't understand but hey, he felt good and that was what mattered.

I held the door open for him. "After you." He went in and as his alpha, I mean, as *an* alpha, and as his date, I was flooded with relief that now he was safe from the cold. Was it a good idea to take him on the nature walk the way I planned?

An older man was a few yards or so away, making his way toward the door. I stood there, holding it.

Chris' blinked at me in confusion. "Teddy. What are you doing?"

"Holding the door." I jerked my head toward the man who was coming up, waiting until he had a hold of the push bar before moving forward. Hadn't Chris seen him? The man nodded his thanks and I gave him the "no problem" nod back.

Chris was grinning as he watched the exchange. I put on a mock frown. "I know that grin. That's the 'Teddy, you're green' grin."

"I'm not laughing at you. You're just really Minnesotan and it's adorable."

Red alert, Chris Chalmers thinks I'm adorable. I dropped my eyes and started stammering immediately. "Th-they don't hold doors where you're f-from?"

"People are assholes where I'm from. Midwest values are refreshing. The real Minnesota Nice."

"The rumors are all true. Although sometimes, it's more like Minnesota Passive-Aggressive." Chris laughed really hard at that, and I preened with pride. "Well, maybe I am a little green. As long as it makes you smile instead of run." His smile softened. That was another look he gave me. Soft and happy, but like he was confused by it, maybe even upset by it. "What's the matter, Chris?"

"Nothing's the matter. Why do you ask?"

"It's just that I'm starting to learn your face. You make a face sometimes, when I say something, I don't know, honest. Like maybe you're not sure if you like it. Am I doing something to make you uncomfortable?"

He shook his head fast. "No, that's not it at all. If you did something that made me uncomfortable, do you think I'd hesitate to tell you?"

That made me chuckle. "Jeez Louise, No way. You'd chew me up and spit me out quicker than I could say 'holy mackerel'." Now Chris was really laughing. I had no idea what I did, but I was proud of doing it. I was so caught up in Chris' smile I forgot we were here to go on a date.

"C'mon, let's get started. I wanna show you the wildlife rehabilitation center."

"Let's do it." Chris looped his arm through mine and my heart palpitated. I'm dying. Hugs, kisses on the cheek, and walking around like we're mates? This was insane. Did that mean that he'd want to kiss me on the lips? My very first kiss, finally, with Chris Chalmers? It would be well worth the wait. I ducked my head and looked away. My face was on fire, and it hurt from grinning. I needed to tread lightly because I was getting a lot of bloodflow down south. If Chris caught the scent of my arousal and that wasn't what he wanted, I would straight-up throw myself into the quaking bog. *Calm down, knot. Now is not the time or the place.* Was I crazy to think the maybe the time would be soon?

"Used to come here a lot," I said to distract myself, "as a kid."

"I can see why. It would be stimulating, with so much to learn. Relaxing, too, with the great outdoors and all." We strolled past the little gift shop toward the hall of displays.

"Exactly. Plus, they had great kids programs. I had a lot of folks looking out for me here. I didn't, uh, I didn't make friends easily." I looked back at the ground.

"*You* didn't make friends easily?" Chris squinted in disbelief. "How? You're so easy to get along with. So...lovable." He smiled, and for a second I was floating on the compliment, until the smile dropped off his face like he just realized something. He let go of my arm and stood a little ways away. He tried not to be obvious about it, but how couldn't I notice when I was tuned in to everything he did like an FM radio?

"Oh. Well, I'm awkward, as you can see. I always say the wrong thing at the wrong time."

"Not with me. It's the opposite, actually." He stuck his hands in his pockets and looked down at the gray carpet, streaked with slush from the kids' shoes and worn down to almost nothing. *Then why are you backing away from me?* "Ooh, what's that?" He pointed at one of the displays. "It says 'please touch'. They're asking for trouble when it comes to my grabby hands." Chris rushed over and picked up an antler. Regardless of whatever just happened, I was still under his spell. I took the opportunity to shake it off. *We're still good. We're still having fun. This is still a million times better than what happened last time.*

Chris turned over a skull in his hands, bleached white by the sun as the animal decomposed on the prairie, a long time ago. "Look at these cool horns! What is this?"

I stepped to the side for a few kids that ran by, their excited shrieks piercing the air. "It's a pronghorn antelope. There aren't any wild ones in the state of Minnesota anymore, only in our zoos."

Chris touched the tip of his finger to the tip of the horn. "Wow. Sharp. You wouldn't wanna tangle with me if I was this guy." He held the skull over the top of his head and pawed at the tracked-up carpet with one foot like he was preparing to charge.

I picked up two deer antlers and held them up like they were growing out of my forehead. "I could take you." So there we were, pawing at the ground, making weird lowing sounds, and pretending to lock horns in the middle of the nature center. My long antlers had a much better reach than his and poked the top of the skull.

"Ow!" He said, as if the skull was really his and he could feel the sharp points. He put a hand over his chest and pretended to stumble backward, mortally wounded. "Uncle!"

I swept back and forth with my antlers, making a big display of it. "I know, right? Look what a tough buck I am. Got you right in the noggin." I was laughing so hard I could barely breath, but I managed to say, "I win?" as I pretended to threaten another charge.

"You win." All the kids in the vicinity thought the "fight" was hilarious, and rushed to take up the antlers and horns, then stage mock fights of their own, as soon as we set them down.

Chris nudged my shoulder with his own. "I'm back to being Chris now. You're not gonna gore me with your antlers right?"

I found enough courage to nudge him back. "You're not challenging the big prairie boss anymore, so you're good to go. As a matter of fact, I'll use my fighting skills to protect you. Make sure you get all the greenest grass and the tastiest tree bark."

Chris winked and gave me that smile that was somewhere between seductive and soft. He leaned into my shoulder, and this time he didn't pull away. "Glad I got myself a big, tough buck to keep me safe." I never considered myself to be big and tough, but with Chris, maybe I could be. *For* Chris, I could be.

He looped his arm through mine again, and my heart did a little jig. Maybe we were back on track. We kept moving through the main atrium and down the hallways, looking at the displays.

"We're coming up to my favorite part." I lowered my voice, remembering the rules in the area.

"What is-" Chris looked up to where a blue and red sign read, "Quiet please, animal rehabilitation in progress."

Chris slapped at my arm. "Really, Teddy?" He whispered, his face close to mine. If I turned my head, I could easily capture his lips in a kiss. My very first kiss.

"You bet. Can't wait until you see what the wildlife center has been able to do." Through the first glass window, in a small, dimly-lit display practically full to bursting with bramble and branches, were two young martens. They darted through the brush so fast, there were only flashes of their little fiery red bodies before they dove into the green again. After that, just disturbances in the brush along with dry leaves rustling.

"There they are," Chris whispered, pointing as they darted back and forth, appearing then disappearing again.

"Look at 'em go. They're so active for this time of day."

"Are they usually not?"

"Nope. Martens are nocturnal." I rattled off some more information about them, like their habitat, what they ate, and what their habilitation process was like.

Chris' eyes were full of wonder as he watched them zip back and forth for a few more minutes, before they disappeared and the branches stopped rattling.

"Never been interested in these little weasel-guys before, but that was cute. I'm learning new things, and I love learning new things."

Wasn't that something? "Me, Teddy Behrens, teaching you, Doctor Chris Chalmers, something new?"

He gave me a gentle punch in the arm. "Stop that, Teddy. You have plenty to teach, and nobody's so smart that they can't learn something new. I'm sure there's a *lot* we could teach each other." His punch turned into a gentle pinch, just firm enough to bite a little. The sensation went straight to my groin. My knot was ready to pop like I was back in junior high, voice just beginning to drop with puberty.

Chris looked over his shoulder at me as he wandered to the next exhibit, exuding a luscious scent laced with arousal.

Mine.

"Way more that you could teach me, that's for sure." I pushed the thought down and followed helplessly to the next display.

What did I do next, though? I had to admit, his signals seemed a little mixed. Was it just me? I was the one who didn't know diddly squat about dating, romance, or sex.

Still, it seemed that at times, Chris was so seductive I had to look down at my pants and say "down boy." Others, he was as sweet as the honeyed center of the chocolates that won him over. As much as seductive Chris had me in a trance, it was sweet Chris that had my heart in his fist.

That time he pulled away from me, though, when he looked so unsure, like he didn't want this, whatever *this* was, those were the times that broke me down, reminded me of all my failures. *Why am I hanging so much on a first date?* I asked myself. The subconscious part of my brain replied, *because this one is special. This one is different.*

"Teddy! Can you tell me about this one?" I brought myself back to reality. Chris had strolled ahead to a different weasel-family enclosure and was waving me over. *Head back in the game, Teddy. Full attention here. Don't fumble the ball.*

I pointed. "With almost all of the enclosures, you'll notice that they start pretty far back from the glass to make it harder for people to disturb the animals by pounding on the glass or smashing their faces against it, you know, all that crazy stuff people do."

"Kids can be rowdy, that's for sure."

"Oh, I'm talking about the parents. They're way worse." Chris pulled a "yikes" face that made me smile. "Some of the enclosures open up in the back, so the animals have the choice of going outside into their habitat. Depending on the species and whether it's ideal for them to be released close to the center, they'll actually start leaving the enclosures open. The animals can venture out, explore, practice finding their own food, and then eventually, one day, they just don't come back."

Chris raised his eyebrows, riveted as we moved on to a bigger display, where the great horned owls were housed. "Never?"

I puffed out my chest, proud that I held his interest with all my animal nerd-speak. "We spot 'em from time to time. It makes us feel good, but the goal is that they go live their lives as normally as possible, and don't go making any more human buddies and depending on them for food and stuff, because that doesn't usually turn out well."

Chris ran a finger over the little information plaque, dry-grass yellow with bright pictures and blocks of red text full of easy-to-digest wildlife facts. "Amazing. This is such important work. I'm glad they're doing it and letting kids get involved."

I stood close to him, purposefully leaning over so one of my shoulders was tucked slightly behind his, giving us a point of physical connection. It was a bold move from me, but I couldn't resist. It felt right. Chris definitely *smelled* right.

I peeked over his shoulder at the profile of his face, his jaw clean-shaven, a hint of a cool aftershave scent mingling with his on the air. "Were you ever into conservation as a kid?"

He chuckled. "Me? No. I didn't realize how important Mother Earth is. I was too into myself."

"Well, you're amazing. I'd be into you to. I mean, I am into you. I mean, if I was you, I'd be into you." Chris pressed his lips together, suppressing what I was coming to know as his "Teddy, you're adorable" smile. His eyes sparkled. *I don't think I could ever get tired of that look on his face.* "Ahem. It's never too late to get into conservation. Folks always think, oh, I'm only one person, what difference is it gonna make? It makes all the difference to one owl, you know? Even if you can only do something like donate five dollars a month. It adds up."

Chris tapped on the plaque with the same fingertip, making a little *thump, thump, thump.* "Sold. The next time I'm near a computer, I'll get these guys set up with a monthly payment. It'll be nice to start giving more back, anyway."

"I didn't mean to imply that you were selfish. After all, you save lives."

He leaned back into me so I was partially supporting his weight. Score one for me being a little bold. "I'm also successful enough that I can comfortably give to important causes. That's how I got a hold of you, right?" He reached across my body, playfully grabbed my forearm, and squeezed.

I lowered my chin so it was rested just slightly on his shoulder. Man, was I ever making big moves today. "That's true. In that case, I think you should give a lot more. Unless it means you go on dates with other alphas. I have to admit that I wouldn't stand in your way, but I won't be a fan."

Chris turned his head to look at me, and again it would have been so easy to have my very first kiss with my dream omega. Chris burst out laughing.

"What?"

"I wish you could see your face right now. You actually looked mean saying that, and I didn't think you could ever look mean."

"The thought of you with another alpha makes me feel kinda mean, to be honest." My instincts rumbled in my chest, ready for a primitive fight to the death for my mate. Would I do that for Chris? Yeah, I would.

"You're so honest."

"My mamas taught me to be an honest boy."

Chris turned his head to look at me again. "They did a good job. They raised a good alpha." From the corner of his eye, he looked over my face, eyes falling to my lips. So close. Closer. Closer. Chris was leaning in. My very first kiss, with Dr. Chris Chalmers.

Mine. Mate.

Here we go.

7

TEDDY

Just as I leaned in, a movement far toward the back of the great horned owl display caught my eye. Someone waving through the glass. My good buddy Dave, from many years ago, was working today. His eyes lit up when he saw me, then he jerked his head back the slightest bit when he saw how close I was to Chris. To kissing him.

I suddenly remembered where I was, and the screams of excited small children filled my ears again. I jumped back from Chris, who gave me a confused look until he followed my gaze and saw Dave back there, looking like the cat who caught the canary. Chris waved to him. Not only was he not ashamed, but he obviously got a kick out of the whole thing. The way Dave grinned had me dropping my eyes, both from bashfulness and from pride that people I knew were seeing me with Chris. However, I didn't get my kiss. Damn it.

Dave made a motion with his hands, his fingers curling toward himself, then pointing at the door, telling me to come in.

It took a second to unstick my tongue and get it working again. "D-do y-you mind if we say hi to my buddy D-Dave? I haven't seen him in a couple of years."

"No problem." Chris held on to my arm, and I led him over to the staff-only entrance and waited.

The heavy metal door, its tan paint chipping around the edges, swung open with a *screeeeeech*. The same hinge that had squealed all those years ago was still doing it.

Dave's ruddy face peeked out.

"Buddy," I said, finally talking to someone I was comfortable poking fun at, "Are we gonna have to have a little conversation about WD-40?"

Dave patted a meaty hand on the door, which made a dull, hollow sound. "You kiddin'? It wouldn't be the same coming in and out on quiet hinges. Gives the place character. C'mere, you old troublemaker." Dave came out with his arms wide. I reluctantly broke contact with my omega, I mean, my date, but I gratefully stepped into the arms of my former mentor.

Dave gave me a few hearty thumps on the back that echoed in my chest cavity. It was a warm and loving feeling. "Good to see ya, pal, it's been too long. Can't have you being a stranger. Now," He turned his smile toward Chris. "Who's this charismatic, attractive person, and what are they doing with the likes of you?"

"Y'know, I've been asking myself the same question," I replied honestly.

Chris held out his hand. "Chris. Great to meet you."

"Pleasure's all mine, Chris. I was just joshin' ya. Teddy here's one of the best guys I know. You can't go wrong with him."

I couldn't read Chris' face when he answered. It was somewhere between affectionate and maybe…confused again? It finally settled on a proud smile. "You know what? I'm starting to see that." I really, really liked that.

Dave crossed his arms and leaned against the door. "What brings you out today, and right on Valentine's Day?"

"O-on a d-date," I murmured, frustrated with myself for stuttering.

Chris patted my chest. "It was a Valentine's Day auction. This guy offered some tasty chocolates and this experience, so I went all-out to get him. Safe to say I'm happy with my results." Chris rubbed my arm and gave me that "I'm gonna eat you alive" look of his. The heat settled in my loins, more intense than before, my knot taking notice of the attention from this one-of-a-kind omega, especially when he was telling other people that he liked me.

Dave put his hands on his hips and rocked back and forth. "That right? I gotta hear more about this, and I'm not quite ready to let you go just yet. C'mon back."

Chris took a tiny step back. "Are you sure? I don't know anything about animals."

"Then I'm gonna teach you. Let's go."

Dave waved us back and we followed him into the series of small, clean, bright rooms. The first held a humble, rickety wooden table for staff to sit at, the same one I used to nap on when I was a tween right before my moms picked me up.

I pointed at it. "Table's still here."

"Probably still has the dent from your forehead." Dave looked at Chris and jerked a thumb at me. "He used to live in this place. He drooled on it so much, his DNA is probably infused with the wood."

Chris laughed, and from the way Dave lapped it up, I knew I was in for a lot more ribbing.

I raised an eyebrow, chuckling. "Is this how we're gonna play it, old man?"

Dave pretended to be offended. "Old man? I'm only like, ten years older than you."

"Try twenty," I said to Chris, which made Dave bluster for a second.

"I'll give you fifteen," he said.

"I know you will," I fired back. I looked at Chris again. "He thinks this is a negotiation or something. Joke's on him, the geriatric patient."

"Hey," Dave protested, but there was no heat behind it.

Chris thought it was all hilarious. He raised his eyebrows and looked me up and down. "Sassy Teddy exists? I never would have thought it."

"Well, I, um…" I stammered, caught out there.

"Oh, he's *plenty* sassy once he settles in. Although probably not with you. Unlike me, he clearly likes and respects you."

"You're turning into a badger in your old age," I shot back. "You look like one, too."

Dave backed into the final room, pointing at me and grinning. "See what I mean?"

"I do see. I like it." Oh, god. My face was on fire and I clenched my fists at my sides so I wouldn't try to cover it up. Was it possible to drop dead from bashfulness? "I like your sweet side even more, though," he added, just for me to hear as Dave forged ahead of us, droning on in his heavy Minnesotan accent about the two latest owls ready to be released.

The final room opened up to a series of big wire cages, full of tree branches, wooden perches, and some with man-made plastic toys for fun and enrichment. A few pairs of wide, wise eyes blinked at us, downy heads swiveling, blinking slowly in curiosity, while a few remained asleep, because this was their bedtime, after all. Memories of working in this very room flooded back to me.

"Most of these beauts will go back into the wild. For example, this little guy here." Dave pointed to an owl who perched in the upper right-hand corner of his closure, peering down at us suspiciously. "Poor guy got stuck in some fishing wire. He mainly needs groceries and to get stronger, and he'll be ready to go. This big gal," he gently tapped on a different cage with an owl who tilted her head at us, just observing with her big golden eyes, "she came in with a broken wing. Once it gets healed up, we're sending her outta here so she can be back in the skies where she belongs." Dave went on to show us more of the owls and some of the other animals that were being rehabbed at the center by the wildlife experts, in conjunction with the kid's program.

Chris was enthralled and kept a strong grip on my arm, squeezing when he got excited. "I can't lie, I never thought owls and animal rehabilitation were all that interesting before, but this is stimulating, and these little guys deserve a second chance."

"For sure," I said, "especially because ninety percent of them are here because of humans."

Chris shook his head slowly. "Terrible. So you used to volunteer here?"

"Sure did," Dave crowed. "He was the best little pooper-scooper I had."

"You scooped poop?"

"Uh huh. I didn't mind it, but there always seemed to be more of a workload with Dave. I guess he was just…giving me shit."

Chris blinked, then he burst out laughing. "Teddy, that was horrible."

"But you laughed," Dave pointed out, undoing the latch to one of the cages. I hadn't noticed, but he'd slipped on a heavy leather glove. When he reached into the cage, a great horned owl stepped onto his arm without a second thought. The little branch he'd been on rattled slightly, the yellowish-green leaves shaking as his huge talons released their iron grip.

Dave pulled him out and he twisted his head around, almost as if showing off the flexion in his neck and his majestic tawny-brown feathers.

"This is Gerald. He's a lifer. He flew too low and tangled with a pickup truck windshield and lost. Bounced right off, apparently. Had a wing injury that didn't heal correctly, so while he does a fair amount of flapping to show everybody who's boss, he can't fly away."

Chris hid behind me, his fingers bunched in the back of my sweater, making the material pull tight across my shoulders. I suppressed a shudder at him pulling at my clothes. *Please, god, don't let Dave smell how turned on I am from Chris pulling at my clothes. I'll never be able to leave the house again.*

I turned and took one of the biggest risks of my life so far; I put an arm around Chris' shoulder. "Hey, there's nothing to be afraid of. The lifers are usually friendly and sweet. We handle them so they get to know and trust us. Let's meet Gerald." We turned back together, my arm around his shoulders. Dave couldn't have been more annoyingly happy about it.

"Oh yeah, this guy's a real sweetheart, don't you worry. Wouldn't hurt a fly." Was Dave talking about me, or Gerald? "If you approach him really slow, he might even let you give him a few strokes." Chris inched forward, keeping one hand on my arm like I was home base as Dave instructed him on the proper way to pet an owl. He skritched Gerald carefully on his chest, lightly ruffling the downy white-and-brown-speckled feathers, and Gerald's beautiful wide eyes blinked blissfully closed.

"Woooooooow," Chris said. "Teddy, get a picture! Get a video!"

"My pleasure." I whipped out my phone and gladly played cameraman. *These pictures are gonna matter. I'm marking the beginning of something here.* That was my wishful thinking and my unruly alpha brain talking to me. *Let's not get carried away, Teddy. But...*

The scene warmed my heart in a brand-new way. Even though so much of this was foreign to him, Chris had stepped into my world with curiosity and enjoyment. That meant everything to me.

I got to pet Gerald, too, and it reminded me of my little buddies from when I was a kid, all gone for some time now.

"Let me take you out back," Dave said, turning around with Gerald perched on his outstretched arm. Gerald's head didn't turn with his body, so his just stared at us with his golden eyes until he got good and ready to face forward.

"So damn cool," Chris whispered as we shrugged our coats on and followed Dave out of the equally squeaky back door.

"The last thing I wanna show you is the enclosures we release them from.

"This is perfect. I was gonna take Chris down to the bog next."

"Oh, he'll love that. That thing's like walking on a waterbed. Plenty of opportunities to fall into each other's arms."

"That right?" Chris asked. He looked like he might be getting *ideas.* Please, let him be getting ideas.

"That's right," Dave said with a nod and a smirk toward me. As if on cue, Gerald stretched his wings and started flapping. On wing was bent at an abnormal angle and didn't fully extend, but it didn't make him any less majestic or impressive. "Whoa! Guess he wanted to show off for you guys today. I think he also wants you to take that walk to see the bog. You better get going, but don't be strangers, got it? Chris, tell Teddy to bring you back for more owl adventures whenever you want. I expect to see you two around."

"You got it, Dave," I said. I was hoping he did have it, and that I'd be seeing Chris enough for us to come back. Chris wasn't objecting, so I took that as a good sign.

Dave gave me one back slap and an "attaboy," and Chris and I started off toward the bog. We had to go downhill, following the well-worn trail between the ankle-high yellow grass that was covered here and there by patches of snow. It wasn't very treacherous, but it required a little vigilance so as not to take a spill.

Chris took my hand, as casually as if it was a regular thing that we just did. I *so* wanted it to be a thing we did. Chris twisted his hands to lace our fingers together. Oh, my god. This was some real hand-holding. Like, not kinda imitating it, but real hand-holding. Not a drill. My feelings toward him were growing quickly, as was my arousal, as was my alpha instinct to claim him as my own. *I'll protect you. I'll never let you fall.*

After a few quick minutes of walking, we reached our destination, a wide open space that one might mistake for a grassland if they weren't careful.

I spread my arms out wide and announced, "This is the bog."

"It's beautiful."

I guided Chris over to the slightly-raised walkway that would lead us through the natural wonder. "It is, right? I never get tired of looking at her."

"What exactly is a bog, anyway?"

I jittered with excitement. This was my time to shine. "A

bog happens in bodies of fresh water when you get an accumulation of decaying plant matter. That's what peat is. Over time, it may even fill in the lake. A quaking bog means the surface is unstable, and it'll sink beneath weight. While this isn't the biggest one, Minnesota does have the biggest peat bog in the lower forty-eight." I rattled off tons of facts, ticking them off on my gloved fingers as we stepped onto the boardwalk, pointing out the aspen, tamarack, and spruce trees that lined the way.

We strolled around, not too slow because it was still cold out, but leisurely enough for it to be a peaceful, sweet late afternoon with the sun lowering in a golden sky. We both fell silent, the only sounds the whistling of the wind through the brush, our light footfalls, and the occasional call of a local critter.

At first, the silence was terrifying. *Gotta fill it. Can't let Chris get bored of me.* Then I realized that he was taking it all in the way I always loved to, the way it was meant to be enjoyed.

The silence became comfortable, just us breathing in crisp air, looking out over Mother Nature's chilled beauty. Something about the moment fostered a natural sense of intimacy, of closeness, even in this wide open space, maybe even because it was a wide open space.

"It means a lot that you brought me here. I wasn't sure what to expect, but you taught me a lot. I'm also getting to learn a lot about you." He gave my coat sleeve a slight tug. "It's great to see the man behind the chocolates, to get a glimpse of who he was as a boy."

I held an arm out. "This explains it. I used to love it here. I learned so much about the animals, helped them to heal, and they were, y'know, safe. Animals don't bully you or tease you or expect you to know what to say all the time. They just trust your energy. They know your heart."

"Teddy," Chris said in a soft voice, "did you get teased a lot as a kid?"

"Did I? I could write the book on it."

"I know kids can be cruel, but what on earth did they find to tease you for? You're like, perfect." He waved a hand at my general everything.

"Me?" My voice was higher-pitched than I would have like when on a date with an omega I was dying to impress, but the Bashfulness Monster reared it's ugly head whenever it wanted. Luckily, Chris always seemed to find it endearing instead of off-putting.

"That's why you got teased, isn't it? Because you're a shy guy."

"That's the long and short of it, yeah. I had one line in my second grade play as Sleepy the dwarf. It took me about five minutes to get it out, I was stuttering so bad. The class had a field day, pointing and laughing. That just made it worse. My teacher even laughed a little herself before she thought to cover it up and save me from myself and the class. I just pretended to actually be asleep the rest of the play, even when I didn't have to. At least I didn't cry until I got home and saw my moms." Remembering that day, even from so long ago, still sliced a nagging little wound in my skin. "They teased me before that, and man, were they bad after that."

Chris rubbed my arm, speaking a little louder to compensate for the cold wind trying to blow his voice away. "I'm sorry you had to go through that. You don't deserve for people to treat your shyness as a bad thing."

"I appreciate it."

"Has it gotten in the way of things for you sometimes?"

"Sometimes." Try all the time. Try ruining my darn life.

"Work, friendships, romance?"

"All of the above." I got a little itchy. We were edging into that territory where things got tricky for me. My mind kept circling back to how my love train had always gotten derailed with other potential love matches. Would that happen with Chris if he found out I was a virgin? The only way to find out was to get that far. I was afraid, but I wanted it more than anything.

"That's too bad. You deserve to have somebody. It's obvious that you're the type who wants something real, a committed relationship full of caring and compassion, and it's crazy to me that you haven't found that yet."

Would it still be crazy if you found out the truth?

I took a deep breath and dove into more of that honesty he praised me for. "I don't know if I should be saying this, or if this is even a real date we're on, but I've waited a long time to be in love, to find that one person that my heart beats for. I want to settle down, get mated, married, have lots of babies, the whole nine yards."

"White picket fence, too?" Chris joked gently, strolling along next to me.

"You bet. A nice little house with a big green lawn for my rugrats to roll around on while me and my mate watch them, tired as hell but happy, sipping lemonade from the porch."

"The simple life. Sounds good. Better than I could have ever imagined." He looked at me, and something like hope shined in his eyes. "For the record, I do think this is a real date. I don't know what the future holds for us, if the future holds anything, but this, this is real."

"Oh," I said dumbly. I couldn't think of a clever reply, so I kept my lips buttoned and kept in step with him.

Chris looked pointedly ahead of us. "You're nothing like the alphas I normally, um, *date.*"

That couldn't be good. "I'm sorry I'm not suave or cool. I'm just little old me, a nurse practitioner from small-town Minnesota."

Chris looked down at the ground, a puzzled, thoughtful frown creasing the corners of his mouth, "No, you're not like them at all. You're not suave or seductive like them."

Ouch. "Sorry, I-"

Chris laughed and waved a gloved hand. "Let me tell you what I mean. You're not suave and seductive like them. You're genuine, where they were all playing a role. It was always a game. I always thought it was all fun and exciting, until, well, it wasn't. You blush and stammer a little and compliment me left and right. It's refreshing to get that honesty in your feelings, straight no chaser. Win, lose, or draw, as much you may not realize it, you're putting it all on the line. Those other alphas never had the balls to do that." He looked back down at the ground and said in a softer voice, "*I* never had the balls to do that."

Hope springs eternal. I sidestepped a big puddle of brown mud frozen over with white frost. As I came back onto the trail, I gently bumped shoulders with him. My arousal was finally taking over, finally handing me a taste of the boldness I'd been lacking my whole life.

I wrapped an arm around his waist. I leaned in close to his ear, my breath coming out in a puff of silver crystalized air, "It's never too late to try." Chris shivered, hard. Jeez. I was trying to be debonair when Chris was suffering from the cold. "Oh no, here I am talking about this crap, and I got you freezing half to death. We don't have to be out here too long if you get too cold."

Chris gave me that "Teddy's adorably oblivious" look. "I know a little something about cold. I'm from Philly."

I scoffed. It was time to be a real Minnesotan. "Oh, ho ho. Maybe you know a *little* something about the cold. You don't know Minne-snow-ta cold."

Chris grinned and leaned his weight on me, making me laugh and stumble a little. "Is this where you lecture me about how you had to walk five miles to school every day in five feet of snow?"

"Uphill both ways, with holes in my boots."

"Oh, shut up." Chris gave me a playful little push, just enough to throw me off balance by a couple of steps. I almost took a tumble onto the bog, but after a little flailing I landed just inside the path with my foot in a small puddle.

Chris' mouth dropped open, laughing as I shook the mud from my boot. "Teddy, I didn't mean to do that."

I chuckled. "Don't worry, these boots are made for walkin'. That doesn't mean I'm not gonna make you pay." There was teasing and a little hint of flirtatiousness in my voice. *Whoa, where's all this coming from, Big Alpha?* I guess Chris brought it out of me. He turned me into someone I didn't recognize, but in the best way.

He lowered his chin and looked at me from below his lashes, as sexy and saucy as ever. "I'd like to see you try." Boy, did that ever rev my engine. For the first time in my life, my alpha instincts jumped out in full, uncontrollable force. *Mate. Claim. Mine.* One second I was being flooded by these new emotions, the next I had sprung forward.

Chris took a couple of steps backward before turning and dashing away, cackling, down the boardwalk. I followed, for once in my life feeling like the conquering alpha, on his way to claim his prize. Chris' scent floated low and heavy, hanging on the cold breeze with the scent of pine.

I chased him for several yards, catching him at a bend in the path, taking us both over the edge to a spot I knew to be safe, only about six inches down onto the solid peat floor. We grabbed on to each other for balance, laughing hard, but I was burning hot despite the weather. Chris smelled a little more spicy, too. A little hotter. A little more like…heat?

I relaxed my hold on him a little, but didn't let go. I just wanted to come back to my senses before I did something out of character, like take him right here and right now.

"Sorry. I got a little carried away. I wasn't myself."

"Don't worry. I love to play games of chase." He hooked a finger under my collar, ran it across the bare skin on my chest. "I love that I riled you up like that."

"You have no idea how much you rile me up. I just don't feel like much of a gentleman not keeping myself under control, chasing you like that."

"That's kinda my goal, Teddy Bear. To make you lose control. Whoa." Chris took a step and felt the ground bow slightly beneath him. It really was like a water bed, and as the patch he was standing on waved with the water below, he surfed it.

"Wuh, whooooa!" He waved his arms in big exaggerated circles, then leaned back and tipped like a falling log. I stepped up to catch him, his back against my chest, wrapped tight in my arms.

He looked over his shoulder at me with that seductive look that was chipping away at my already-feeble willpower.

"Look at that," he whispered. "You caught me after all. My hero."

I was finally catching on. "You did that on purpose."

"Oops. What gave me away?" He obviously wasn't sorry at all. The bog roiled again, just slightly with so much of the plant matter frozen. Chris leaned his head farther back, resting his cheek on my shoulder, tucking his face into my neck. He nuzzled lightly, his nose in the short beard on my jawline, his lips ghosting over the tender skin of my neck. I held my breath, and tried to hold my knot, as Chris leaned back to look me in the eye, smiling like a predator that had its prey back into a corner. In our little games of cat and mouse, there were times that I'd played the hunter, but I was glad to let Chris eat me alive.

He tilted his chin up. I tilted mine down. Our lips slowly neared each other as I held him in this beautiful frozen landscape, just the two of us. Finally, our kiss.

Mother Nature had other ideas.

Chris readjusted his footing so he could push up a little more and get the right angle to kiss me. Unfortunately, a little pool of water had accumulated right where his foot landed. His foot went in and hit mud with a *squelch*.

"Shit," he cursed, as winter-cold water covered his foot.

"Sugar," I said, trying not to curse.

It made Chris laugh a little as he hopped on one foot, trying to shake some of the water off. It was much too late for that, though. "At least I can count on you to be cute through all this."

"We gotta get you someplace warm immediately. Cold water plus toes plus freezing weather equals disaster." I grabbed him by his waist and swept him up off the ground, hitting a fast jog back toward the building, careful of the slippery terrain.

"Okay, let's go-oooooo!" Chris yelled, waving a fist in the air. He whooped and hollered the whole way back to the visitor center, so even though I was sick to death that he'd catch cold, it was still a lot of fun.

Back inside, it was much more calm and quiet, as all of the children had left for home by then.

"You can put me down now," he teased.

"No, I can't," I huffed.

"You ran me up a hill."

"I dropped you in a puddle, it's the least I can do."

"What a gentlealpha. Excuse me while I swoon." I took him into the event room where our romantic dinner set-up was already waiting, complete with white taper candles throwing off gentle firelight and a bottle of champagne on ice.

Chris gasped as I carried him into the room. "I love it."

I was panting from the exertion but trying to hide it to impress him. "You do?"

"Of course, I do."

"We'll take care of your feet first, then we'll have at it, okay?"

His voice was breathy as he watched me crouch down in front of him. "Okay."

I peeled off his shoe and his sock and I examined his foot in my hands. The cold of his skin was a shock to the skin of my hands, but I was fully aware of how intimately I was touching him.

"Doesn't look like there was time for any frostbite to set in. Can you feel it when I wiggle your toes?" I gave each one a little pinch, just enough to send an electrical signal to his brain saying all the neurons were firing down there. He bit his lip and nodded. "What about if I squeeze here?" I pressed my thumb into the ball of his foot. Chris let out a throaty moan.

I sat up straighter. "Did that hurt?"

"Hurt?" He chuckled. "No, indeed."

"Okay, good. Let me just rub them a little more to make sure there's blood flow." I pressed more firmly and he squirmed. "Thought it didn't hurt, Chris?"

His voice came out husky and low. "It doesn't, baby. Feels good. Keep going." Baby. Did he realize he just called me that? How was I ever supposed to go back to life the way it was before he called me baby?

I focused on his feet instead of the raging desire building up from my toes. Chris wasn't helping my cause, letting out little sighs and moans as I worked. He sounded like this when he made love, didn't he? I'd kill to know. If I wasn't mistaken, that spicy scent of his arousal was real, and growing stronger. Could he possibly be on the edge of a heat?

I huffed soft, warm breath on his toes, just to make sure they'd be okay. I didn't realize he would react with more of his patented sexiness.

"Yes. I like that, Teddy."

"Oh, okay, yeah, that's great, I think we're great." I placed his foot gently on the ground and hopped to my feet. *Break time, Teddy, before you get yourself in too deep.*

I gave him my socks and examined his waterlogged shoes, just to have something to distract me from the slighty-swelling knot in my pants. "These are gonna need to be cleaned. Do you want me to get these cleaned?"

Chris shook his head, a little rueful. "Don't worry about it. They're ruined."

I held a hand to my mouth. "Oh, no. I ruined my date's shoes. This wasn't a good idea at all."

Chris chuckled and laid a hand on my bicep. "Teddy, stop that. I knew what I was getting into when I chose to come on this date with you. I also knew better than to wear those shoes in the first place, but there were two different things at play."

I scrunched my brow in confusion. "What were those?"

Chris shifted in his seat a little, back to that weird hint of being ill-at-ease. I didn't think an omega like this, who could have anything and anybody he wanted served right up on a platter, could even *be* ill-at-ease. That was for awkward people like me.

"You've been so open with me about your thoughts and feelings. Can I be honest?" He bit his lip, unsure.

"You betcha, Chris. You can shoot straight with me." *Please don't let this be him shooting me down, though.*

Chris laughed, and the smile put me at ease. "You really are from Minnesota, aren't you?"

"Gee golly gosh, you don't know the half, pal." That sent him into a laughing fit, and I'd keep the Minnesota-isms coming to keep him laughing like that. I wasn't good with cracking jokes, so to get a laugh, especially from my dream guy, was a high like no other. "Just be careful not to bump into me. Then I'll be forced to break out the 'ope, lemme just slide right by ya.'" That really had him laughing, and I just took it all in.

Mine, my archaic alpha brain thought. That was an inappropriate and outdated way of thinking, but my base instincts just *wanted*, and for once in my life wasn't it good to just *want*? "What, uh, what were the two things?"

Chris dropped his eyes, hesitating. For the first time, he wasn't in total control. It was intriguing to see behind the wall. I liked it, shy, somewhat unsure Chris Chalmers. That I'd made him that way? The icing on the cake.

"First, I wore these shoes because I really wanted to impress you."

That was a shock. I poked my finger into my chest. "Impress me? Anything you do impresses me, you didn't have to put in any effort at all." It was stuff like that that made me sound kinda lame.

Before I could regret it, Chris squeezed my arm, acknowledging my feelings. "There you go, being vulnerable, telling the truth in a way I've always been afraid to."

"I'm just surprised, you know? And I say the first thing that comes to my head because I don't know how to package it different, or lie, or play it cool, I guess?"

"I like that about you."

Hot prickles covered my body, in a good way. "You said you wanted to impress me, but, why would you wanna do that?"

Chris bit his lip, one corner of his mouth curling up. "I guess that brings me to the second thing. The reason I wanted to impress you was the same reason I'm mad at myself for landing in the puddle. I don't want the date to end. I'm having so much fun with you. I *like* you."

I repeated that back slowly, trying to wrap my mind around it. "*You* like *me.*"

Chris gave me a secret little smile. "Yeah, I do."

I put my hands on my hips and shifted my weight to one foot. "Jeez Louise, you gotta be joshin' me."

"You're just doing that on purpose now!" Chris said. He wrapped his arms around his stomach and honest-to-god giggled. It was sweet. Chris was a lot of things: sexy, talented, self-assured, charming. Sweet, I wouldn't have added to the list until now. Sweet, just for me? All these secret sides of him, I wanted just for me. *Here I go wanting again. Mine.*

Chris' scent was even more receptive now. Sweet like honey, with a hint of something spicy and warm. It turned me on something fierce, brought something out of me that wasn't even human, just a collection of sensory information that took my omega's scent and close proximity to mean it was time to mate. Time to make babies. *Cool it, Teddy. You're not a barbarian. If Chris wants that with you, he'll be loud and clear about it. It seems like we're headed that way, though. He's been flirting, right? He says he likes me, right?* Likes *likes me?* Then maybe. Nothing was impossible. Love, mating, marriage, a baby, none of that was off the table, even if I was a psycho for thinking that far ahead with this guy on the first date. How could I help it when Chris was just so...Chris?

"Can you help me up?" He held his hands out. I learned fast that one of my favorite things to do was help Dr. Chris Chalmers stand up, because it was the best excuse in the world to hold his hand.

When I helped Chris out of the chair, the same sparks flew that had flown the first time they announced him as the winner at the auction. It was so strong, I was sure I'd never feel anything stronger for anyone else, and that this would never fade.

Chris was standing, but we weren't going anywhere. We were face-to-face, only a couple of inches apart, since that's where Chris ended up once he got to his feet. We'd been holding hands the whole time, and Chris gazed deep into my eyes, his face illuminated by candlelight, just as intense as always. It overwhelmed me, being the object of such an omega's focus. He was the sun and as much as I wanted to look directly at him, witness his power and beauty, he burned my eyes out in the best way.

Chris leaned in, getting closer and closer. Were his lips puckered? It looked like it, but maybe I was imagining things with all the starts and stops and my desperation. I didn't wanna get this wrong; if I had my wires crossed I'd ruin my chance with my dream omega. If he *did* want to kiss me...that was even scarier. I'd dreamed for years about what a kiss would feel like. If it was anything like the movies, feeling how I felt about Chris, I'd catch fire and burn from the top down.

I was now officially rock hard, my erection straining against my jeans. I couldn't help myself, but I was still so unsure. I needed to hear Chris say he was coming on to me. He'd tell me, after all.

Turned out, he did.

He closed the gap between us, pressing his body against mine, his warmth penetrating through both our layers of clothing. His scent was insane. I hadn't spent a heat with an omega before, my alpha lizard brain had set off a screaming yellow siren. "You know, I've been wanting to kiss you all day."

"Y-you have?" I thought it was just my imagination. My heart kicked off a one hundred meter dash in my chest. "M-m-m-me, too."

"Good. I thought so." Chris rested his fingertips on my cheeks. The touch was light, but each point felt like a revelation. I raised my shaky hands and rested them on his hips. He pressed his groin into me, and there. He was hard, too. And was that...slick I scented? An ugly *hngggh* noise slipped out of my mouth as I held myself off from ejaculating in my pants.

"May I?" He asked softly. There was nobody around, nobody to interrupt us. No reason not to have my first kiss with Dr. Chris Chalmers. I let my eyes fall closed. If he didn't kiss me, I was gonna drop dead on the spot. Hell, if he *did* kiss me I'd probably still drop dead.

"Please," I whispered, bracing myself for the sensation. My lips pursed in anticipation as Chris slowly, so slowly, closed the gap between us.

8

CHRIS

TEDDY LOOKED AT ME LIKE HE WAS GOING TO DIE IF I DIDN'T KISS him. Judging by the way I'd been gravitating to him the whole afternoon, his kindness, his attentiveness, his bare, pure soul, helpless to his pull no matter what I tried, if I didn't kiss him I might die, too.

So what was I so afraid of? *There's nothing to be afraid of. It'll just be a kiss, like every other kiss you've had before.* As I lied to myself, my conscious whispered, *you know what the truth is, Chris. Mate. Mine.*

I might have been fighting those thoughts, but there was no more fighting the need for Teddy that had taken over my body, and threatened to take over my heart. I tilted my head and gave him a soft press of my puckered lips. He kissed back, his fingertips under my shirt, digging desperately into the flesh of my hips, just enough to hurt.

I pulled back an inch to look at him. He looked shocked, but not like he'd seen a ghost. Like he'd seen an angel.

"Finally," he whispered. "Finally." Kissing Teddy wasn't like kissing anybody else at all. It was like the first time.

I couldn't stand to have him look at me like that. I couldn't stand not to kiss him again.

This time, I parted his lips with mine, slipping my tongue inside, making the kiss deep and wet and slow. Teddy wrapped his arms around my waist and practically pulled me right off my feet, pulling me as close to him as humanly possible. Shy-guy Teddy was clearly inexperienced, but what he lacked in technique he more than made up for in enthusiasm and red-hot passion. I led the kiss and he followed eagerly, quickly adapting and learning until the kiss was good, then damn good, then, *I gotta get him home right now.*

Teddy clasped his forearms behind my back and squeezed, cradling me like I was the most precious thing in the world. As our tongues danced together, I realized this *was* the first time. I'd never really kissed an alpha before Teddy Behrens. This was different.

I needed more, much more. I slipped a hand down to his thigh, trailing my fingers up until…

Crash! Teddy and I jumped apart at the sound. In the doorway was a startled server in a white button-down and black slacks, juggling silverware and two covered dinner plates on a serving tray, trying not to drop it. When he got everything righted, he breathed a huge sigh of relief.

"Sorry, I'm so sorry," Teddy ran over to him, apologizing profusely.

The server, who clearly knew Teddy, went from shock and panic to mischievous. "It's okay. I didn't expect for you to be doing, ahem, what you were doing, but I'm glad to see it, Teddy."

Teddy dropped his eyes in that bashful way of his, but he

also looked a little smug, a little proud. "Thanks, man." He looked over to me. "Hey, so, I, uh, I think dinner is ready. We should, like, sit down and eat it and stuff."

The server laughed out loud. "Dude, are you serious right now?"

"What?" Teddy asked, holding his hands up in confusion.

The server laughed and shook his head slowly. "This guy. It's cute how oblivious he is, right?"

"Downright adorable," I replied. "I like it."

"Apparently, you do."

"And he's about to find out how much."

The server looked back at Teddy and winked. "Love that for you, my friend."

"Love what for me?"

I laughed out loud. The dinner smelled delicious, savory and rich and flavorful, but I had something in front of me I wanted to eat much more. "Wanna take this dinner to go?"

Teddy squinted, and I could practically see him doing the math in his head. When the light bulb went off his eyes popped open. "Oh! Yes. I do, yes. More than anything. Let's go."

"I have boxes," the server said, turning and heading for the door with the silverware rattling on the tray. "I'll put this in boxes."

"Hey, uh, could you, uh, hurry?" Teddy said.

"You got it, buddy." He power-walked out of the door.

I pushed up against Teddy again, enjoying the turned-on-deer-in-headlights look on his face. "Where were we?" I slid the hand back up his thigh, hearing his breath hitch as I ran my palm over his bulge. His quite generous bulge. I wanted to feel that so bad. "That's right. We were right here." Teddy gasped and rocked forward on his toes until I was cupping him through his jeans. He bit his lip, hissing helplessly as I toyed with him, teased him.

"I'm coming in again," came a voice from right outside the door.

I whipped around and pressed my back up against Teddy's front. "We're decent!" I called. "Well, mostly," I whispered to Teddy, rubbing my ass lightly over his crotch. He tightened up, trying not to show how turned on he was, but it was obvious by his scent. Potent, pure, strong alpha, but with a hint of sweetness.

The server hustled in with a couple of big white paper bags with a logo on them, the delicious smell still wafting out. It couldn't match Teddy's though.

"Whoa," he said with a laugh, jerking back a little. Clearly, he'd walked into the perfume cloud our of scents. "Here everything is, and I'm gonna get out of your hair. You both have a greeeeeeat night." He gave me a pointed look. Teddy dropped his face into my shoulder.

"We will," I promised, arching my back up just enough so the server didn't see it but Teddy felt it.

Once he was gone, Teddy grabbed the food in one hand and my hand in the other. "For the love of god, let's get outta here."

"Let's."

We held hands, giggling, as we jogged to his car. The weather was freezing, every exhalation a puff of white air that floated up into the moonlight, but it couldn't cool us down.

We stole more kisses in the front seat like teenagers, kissing and kissing until Teddy pulled up for air.

"We're frosting the window." There was a beautiful crystalline pattern blooming at the bottom of the windshield and working its way up.

"So?" I asked, diving in for more kisses.

Teddy reluctantly pulled away to start the car, its engine slowly turning over with a frozen *whur-whur-whur.* He flipped the heat switch, with blasted us with chilly air, and hit a black button that lit up when he pressed it. "Defrost," he said. "Can't drive us home if I can't see."

I cursed. "Good point."

"Plus, your shoes."

"Oh." I looked down at them dumbly and suddenly there was the shock of cold seeping in on my toes. "I forgot."

"I made you forget?" He asked, ducking his head to hide that bashful smile of his.

"You sure as hell did." If not for the cold, more than enough to literally freeze our asses off, I might have taken things to the backseat. I was glad for it, though, when Teddy started the windshield wipers and the thin, slighty-melted frost came off with a few swipes. I wanted someplace much more special than a backseat for our first time together.

He backed out and we got on the road. I touched everything in my reach, sliding a hand across the width of his shoulders, down his arms, back up his thigh. Back to the sweet spot. I gave his dick a healthy squeeze and he yelped, swerving a little. The road had small patches of ice so we slid a few more inches than we were comfortable with before the car righted on the road.

"Maybe I'd better cut that out until we're out of the car."

"Wouldn't be a bad way to die," Teddy said with a chuckle.

"Settle for holding hands for now?"

"Deal." We interlaced our fingers and let them rest on the black leather of the center console, still a little cold from the car sitting outside all day. Though the air in the cabin was charged with sexual tension, it was nice to just hold Teddy's hand like this, stroking my thumb over his. It was cold, but overall I was still so hot. I tugged at the collar of my sweater and pulled my coat zipper down a few inches with my free hand.

"You hot already, honey?" He asked, his eyebrows scrunched in concern. *He called me honey.* I was even hotter now. I did slip up and call him "Baby" earlier. Those sorts of words just flowed out of my mouth around him, I couldn't help it.

"Yeah, nothing to worry about, my layers are just working better than expected, I guess."

Or maybe Teddy was sending me into heat. I was slicking the nice pants I wore on the date. He turned me on like hell and he was so sweet he made my teeth ache. My very own honey-dripping heartthrob.

If I was going into heat for him, did I really wanna fight it? *No,* my heart said. *If I'm going into heat for him, I want to get lost in it.*

Luckily it was only a ten-minute drive to his place, a cute, simple little one-level post-war rambler. Teddy parked in front of it and ran around his car to open the door for me. As soon as he pulled me out I leapt at him, kissing him again full-force. We made out in his driveway until the cold and possible prying eyes of neighbors drove us in. I wasn't feeling the Minnesota-cold anymore because my body was now a radiator.

Teddy opened the front door for me and held out an arm for me to go in front of him. "This is it."

"It's so cute." It was simply decorated with floral-patterned couches and pops of soft pastels on the wall.

"Thanks, I, uh, let my Mama decorate. She had a good time."

"That's so sweet." Could this alpha stop being so earnest? He was just fanning the flames of the wildfire.

As soon as the door clicked shut behind him, I grabbed the front of Teddy's coat with both hands, turned him around, and pushed him up against the door with a dull *thud*. Teddy threw his hands up against the wall like he was under arrest. I laid my hottest, sexiest kiss on his lips.

"Mmph," he moaned into it. Again, I carefully coaxed him into massaging my tongue the way I wanted. Teddy was a fast learner and soon he wasn't just taking what I had to give him, he was volleying back and forth with me like we were on a tennis court.

In a surprise twist, he turned me around and pushed me up against the wall. It shook something loose in me, and suddenly I was sopping wet, the insides of my thighs damp with hunger for this alpha. I gaped at him with surprise.

His cheeks pinked up. "Always wanted to do that." He dove back in for another kiss like he needed the practice. He was already better at it, and by the time the kiss ended, my knees were knocking together, rattling like maracas.

"Bedroom?" I whispered, tearing at his coat, yanking it off his shoulders.

He hesitated. "Uh, yeah. Yeah."

Hmm. Maybe I was imagining the hesitation. It was hard to be sure, because my brain was foggy with my omega desires. "Lead the way."

Time ticked by so slowly, it must have taken another year to get into his bedroom. His bed was huge and covered with fluffy blankets. Lots of room for what we were about to do.

I tackled him onto the bed and we fell back, giggling. "Teddy, after those kisses, I gotta have you. Strip." Teddy leaned back just the slightest, but it was enough to let me know something was off. "What's the matter? You don't wanna do this?"

"What? No! Of course I do." For once in my life, I found myself second-guessing what I just did. There was something about Teddy that made me just care more.

"Was I too aggressive? I know some alphas don't like that."

"Are you kidding? I love that you're aggressive. Or else, how would I have known you like me?" He looked down at the blankets, scratching the back of his head.

"Damn right, I like you. I'd like you to be inside me, too."

Teddy stammered. "Oh, my gosh. I was kinda hoping, but I wasn't sure, I didn't think, um, what, uh, comes next?"

I turned my sexy eyes on full blast and gave him *the look.* My heat was coming on full-blown, and I needed my alpha right now. Wanted his knot. "What do you want to come next?"

Sweat beaded at Teddy's hairline. "We could maybe kiss some more? Then after that, you tell me what you might like, or, want, or…" He looked off, rambling a little.

Something was off about his body language.

I drew back into myself a little. Why would I be sensitive to what's going on, even if something was wrong? I was never out to take advantage of my sexual partners, but I wasn't very open to them emotionally, either. Wham, bam, thank you, alpha. "Teddy, is there something wrong?"

"No!" He said, too loud and too fast. "There's nothing wrong. No problem."

Through the steam of my heat, I could still make out that there was more to the story. I laid a hand on his chest, just above his heart. It beat wildly under my palm. "If something's going on, you gotta tell me. We can't go any further until we clear the air."

For a second, Teddy looked like he might explode. The next, he took a deep breath and launched. "It's my first time."

I narrowed my eyes at him. "What's your first time." It came out as a statement instead of a question.

He gestured toward the room at large. "This. All of this."

I wasn't computing. "You've never had sex in your own bed before?"

"No, I've never…" He tilted his head to the left and the right, then used one hand to indicate the length of my body. "You know."

The shock hit me like a meteor. "You've never had sex at *all?*"

Teddy slapped a hand over his eyes and dropped back on his bed with a little bounce. "No, and I've never done what we just did."

I couldn't get any more shocked if I tried. I leaned a hand against the headboard to support myself.

"You mean to tell me you're a virgin?" He nodded, keeping his eyes covered. "You've never had sex and you've never been kissed." He shook his head. I stared, mouth hanging open like a Venus fly trap. "Ever?"

Teddy frowned. "Yeah. I mean, it just kinda, hadn't happened yet, you know? I tried all the time, but I don't know why. Maybe because I'm too-"

I waved a hand through the air. "Whatever it is you're about to say, don't. It's probably something negative where you're trashing yourself for being different again. Whatever you think kept you a virgin, and whatever reason you have to think being a virgin is a bad thing, it's all wrong." Teddy's lip trembled and his face creased with awe, like I was a celestial body who floated down from heaven.

"Really?"

"Really."

"It's just that I've wanted to be with someone like this, but I've always been so, so *me*, and I wanted it to be special, with someone special, and the longer I went without even being kissed, the more I felt like a freak."

I rested a finger on his lips. "Listen to me. You're not a freak. First of all, there are tons of people who don't start having sex until later in life. It's normal and it's nothing to be ashamed of. Second, I think it's wonderful that you wanted your first time to be special. I wish I had that mindset when I was younger." I wished I had that mindset even a few months ago. "Third, you're special. You're special to me." I let that hang in the air for a second. I didn't want to acknowledge how much I meant it. "If you wanna go for a fourth, technically, there's no such thing as 'virginity.' It's a societal construct."

Teddy just stared at me. With his sweet adoration focused on me like that, I might as well have had a billion dollars in the bank for how rich I felt.

"Keep looking at me like that and you won't be a virgin much longer," I joked.

"Okay," Teddy whispered, his lips moving softly against my finger, his breath ghosting over the tip.

I was so slicked up and ready I could hardly stand it. "Teddy, I think there's a little more at play here. I think you sent me into heat."

"I did? You've been smelling soooo good." He pulled me close to him and took a long whiff, running his nose upwards on the center of my breastbone. "No wonder I'm feeling so out of control. It's you, and your heat on top of that. A force of nature."

"You want to do this with me? Tonight?"

"I can't *not* do this with you tonight."

"I just want you to be sure."

"Never been more sure about anything in my life." He held my chin between his thumb and forefinger and kissed me softly. Once again, we made out. This time I slipped a leg over his waist and straddled him in a smooth, practiced motion. Teddy lay there like he was pinned in place, so I took his hands in mine.

"What is it, honey?"

"It's just," he gulped, his throat bobbing, "I'm nervous. I want to please you."

I cupped his chin in my hand. "You will." I held the hem of his shirt between my fingers. "May I?"

"Yes. Please." He lifted his arms. I pulled the shirt over his head and revealed his body, a work of art if I'd ever seen one. Solid with lean muscle. Not defined, but not needing to be. Just built strong.

"Can't believe nobody's ever enjoyed this before me. It's insane. The people who made you feel unwanted, they were crazy, you know that? But I'm here now."

"Okay," he whispered. I had no idea why I was saying all these things to him like we were in love. It was getting harder and harder to stay sensible in this heat, to remember my own rules.

"I want to take care of you, do this thing right. Do you mind if I take control?" He quickly shook his head. "Okay. I want to kiss you all over. Can I?" Teddy nodded even faster, eager.

I was ready to take over, to possess my alpha- no, not mine. But he was giving up all control and letting me take care of him.

I wanted to make this alpha's body mine. So I did.

9

CHRIS

I started with his cheeks, his forehead. Being in heat made my body want to rush, but this needed to be special for him. *It needs to be special for you, too, Chris.* I ignored that.

I kissed his jaw gently, then lower, over his throat. Teddy hissed as I gave his skin a touch of tongue, right on his pulse point. I leaned back up and kissed behind his ear, adding the tip of my tongue there, too, just a little wet heat. Teddy writhed beneath me, his fingers clutching the sheets, bunching the thin cotton up between his fingers.

I did the same to the other side of his neck, his other ear, before working my way down his chest. I traced a long, slow, glistening trail with my tongue before paying each nipple some attention, giving each one a lick and light nibble between my teeth. They pebbled and hardened for me and Teddy swore, gripping the sheets harder.

"Sensitive there, are we?" I teased.

"You're driving me crazy."

"Good." *I'm pleasing my alpha.* Ugh. I wasn't gonna get my

heat to calm down and stop crossing the wires between love and lust anytime soon, so once again, I ignored it. I had to focus at the task on hand, anyway. I kissed down Teddy's stomach, running my hands up his obliques.

His body stiffened as I reached the trail of hair that led down to his happy place.

"Not yet, Baby," I whispered, drinking his groan of lustful agony.

"Gonna kill me, honey."

"No, I won't," I reassured him with a laugh as I squeezed his muscled thighs. "It'll just feel that way." He chuckled until I kissed the inside of his thigh, then he hissed and jerked. I buried my nose in the crease of his groin, enjoying the heady scent of this alpha. My alpha. Mine.

I kissed my way down one leg and up the other, dragging my tongue up, agonizingly slow, until I again reached his center. I wrapped my hand around the base of him, thick and heavy in my hand.

"Ooh, all this for me?"

"Yeah- Oohhhhh," Teddy moaned as I jerked him slowly, twisting my hand around the crown of his cock.

He threw his forearm over his eyes, his hips jerking with every movement. "Chris I, I can't hold it."

"That's okay. You did so good. Wanna see you let go." As soon as I gave Teddy "permission," he thrust his hips up into my fingers, frantically, and came in my hand, the flushed head of his cock shooting ropes of hot seed all over my hand, even getting some on my chin.

"Whoa," he whispered after he caught his breath. "That was incredible. Look at you with-" He snapped his jaw shut and stared at me with lines of semen on my arm and face. *Yes, mark me, make me yours. My alpha.* Nope, I couldn't think like that.

"You did good," I joked.

He looked down at his manhood, still pulsing in my hand. "I'm still hard."

"Sex with an omega in heat will do that to you." Not to mention an omega you shared a deep connection with, even after just one date, but I wasn't talking about that.

"It'll do what, turn me into Superman?"

I dropped my face into his thigh and laughed. "I can't believe how cute you are."

"What about you? Wanna please you."

"Oh. Yeah, I-" I looked down and my dick was throbbing between my legs, neglected and hard as rebar.

"Can I, can I taste you?"

"Absolutely." Chris reached out a hand for me and I knee-walked up, straddling him again. He pulled me closer until I straddled his chest. I tried to roll off, but he held me in place, wrapping a hand around me this time, lifting his head to watch his hand work me over. Dear god, did it ever feel good.

Teddy stroked me, grinning like a kid on Christmas morning. "Just like this is good. It's hot. Like in the pornos sometimes."

I cackled, rocking my hips into his grip, breathless. "You get that porn is not real sex, right?"

"For sure. There are just some things I thought looked hot, but figured I'd never get to try 'em."

"It's your night, sweetheart, and I'm gonna enjoy myself so have at it."

"Would you tell me how to do it? Just so I do it right."

I thumbed at his cheek, his light stubble scratchy under my thumb. "Of course I will." I applied the slightest pressure to his bottom lip, until he parted them enough for me to slip my thumb in. "Open your mouth nice and wide, stick your tongue out for me, baby…that's it." I rested my length on his tongue, between his lips, all pretty and pink and moist. I pushed forward carefully so as not to choke him, but it was hard to restrain myself as I sank into the tight suction of my alpha's mouth. *No, not my alpha.*

"Just go back and forth on it, and suck as you pull your head back, like a popsicle. Yeah, that's it, Teddy, you're so good."

Teddy hummed around me, then pulled off just long enough to say, "You taste so sweet, like a popsicle. Yum." I laughed a little, but I was too busy being carried away by lust.

I reached around and slid a finger inside myself. It was damn good, having something in me, taking the edge off my burning need to be penetrated, but it wasn't nearly enough. Only a teaser. Only Teddy could fulfill my needs now.

"Gimme your hand, babe." I clasped one of the hands he had on my thigh and guided it between my legs. I slipped his fingers into my cleft, guiding them where I needed them the most. Teddy's fingers replaced mine. I guided his wrist so he was fucking me in time with my thrusts into his mouth, my slick running into his palm and down his wrist.

Chris moaned around my girth, sucking with more enthusiasm.

"Not too hard, baby, just…" He lowered the pressure in his suction a little and hit perfection. "Like that, just like that. God, look at you." He gazed up at me from beneath his eyelashes. He grinned with my length stretching his cheeks, filling his mouth. "How do you still look so innocent like that?" He full-on shrugged, which made it even cuter. I couldn't take it any more. I had to feel him breaching my rim.

"Time for the main event, okay?" He nodded and I slipped out of his mouth with a wet pop. "Don't move, just stay right there." I wriggled down until I was hovering over his dick. I moved his hands to my waist as I sank down on him, taking care because he was, indeed, well-endowed, gasping at the stretch, my thighs straining from holding myself up.

Finally, I sank all the way down, Teddy's shaft inside me deep, touching all the parts that made me spark and fizz.

Teddy was breathless. "Wow." He looked at where our bodies joined, just barely discernible in the dim light. "Wow. Really, wow."

I winked. "Don't worry, it gets better."

"It does?" I chuckled and motioned my hips forward. Teddy cursed. "Sorry, it's just...wow. Can you, um, hold on for a second?"

I covered my grin with a hand. "No problem, but I won't be mad if you don't last. I think I went a whole forty-five seconds dry-humping my first boyfriend before I came in my pants, and you took that tongue bath really well."

"That makes me feel a little better," Teddy gritted out. "Can you, um, go again, please?"

"My pleasure." At first I rode him slow and smooth, but soon I couldn't keep my composure. I bounced my ass on his dick, showing him just what I could do. Chris didn't hold back with showing me how good it was.

"Yeah. Yeah. Oh my god, Chris, sex is so good. Sex with *you* is so good. You're amazing. This is the best. This is- Oooooooohhhhhh." He got loud when I ground down on him, tried to bring him closer to the edge.

"I want your knot," I whispered in his ear. "Come on, Teddy. Give it to me, come on." Teddy kept one hand on my waist but threw the other above his head, his neck arched, veins bulging as I rode him. After a time, he gripped me tighter and pulled me down to meet his shallow upward thrusts. It took a second to catch a rhythm, but when we did and Teddy fucked up into me in earnest, it was lights-out.

"I'm, oh god, I'm close to…" he bit off his words.

I slowed my pace down. "Can you hold it, baby? Just for a second so I can come with you?" He squeezed his eyes shut tight and nodded, looking like he was on a torture rack but loving it. I'd have to leave the discussion about edging for another time. "Don't worry, baby. I'm close, too. Just hang on with me, just for a little while, and we can come together. Then I want that knot in me."

"You can't talk like that, then," he said with a breathless chuckle, the base of his cock already swelling in me. God, it was gonna be big. I tightened my grip around his hand around my length. I fucked into his fist as I rode him, hard, hard, hard. His headboard knocked against the wall, *bang, bang, bang.*

Teddy's nails dug furrows in my skin, little pinpricks of pain that heightened my pleasure. "Chris, I'm gonna, can I, please…"

"Yeah. Come for me, Teddy. You've been so good for me, so good." Teddy erupted, his back arching, lifting me up off the bed, grinding impossibly deeper, his knot swelling, bigger, and bigger, and bigger.

"God, your knot. I don't know if I can take it." From his wide eyes, it was clear he was about to freak out. "Don't worry. I will. I just need some time to get used to it, baby. You got me so filled up."

Teddy groaned, and filled me up even more with his hot cream. "You can't just *say* stuff like that, hun. Jesus."

I cackled like the evil villain I was. "Why not?" Then I yelled, "oh, god," and I was coming. My mouth opened in a silent scream and my toes curled and my nervous system lit up with all the good electrical signals and yes, I was coming on my mate's knot, yes, *yes…*

When I finally regained my senses, I'd spent myself on his belly.

Teddy was thrilled about it. "Nice."

I collapsed forward on him, at least as much as I could with him stuck inside me. *My alpha.* "Nice, indeed." I adjusted my legs, getting settled in because we were gonna be there for a while.

I rested my hands on his pecs as we talked. It was forty-five minutes before Teddy's knot went down enough to release me.

"Ahhhh," I let out a long, relaxed breath as I rolled off of him. "I was starting to cramp so bad."

We laughed at that. The problem was, now I felt empty. More. More sex, more knotting, more of my alpha. Mine.

Heat-sex brain was making it hard to think. The plan was to only have sex with Teddy one time, just to get it out of my system, but the exact opposite had occurred. Now sex with Teddy was *in* my system. Even if I wasn't in heat, I'd be howling for more. Can I count my heat as just one time? That makes sense with how crazy heat sex makes you. Yeah. This is just once, that's all. All lies, but I ignored the nagging in my heart about it.

I better share this thought with Teddy, make sure I don't get his hopes up if he wanted to see me again. Would he want to see me again? How are you so insecure about this Chris? You just rocked that alpha's world!

He took my hand and kissed my knuckles gently. "This was wonderful. Better than my wildest dreams. Thank you."

"No, thank you." It felt like my first time. It was my first time. Whether I was willing to admit that or not was another matter.

"That was, that was…" The grin that spread over his face was euphoric. "It was the best ever. When can we do it again?"

"Right now."

My heat took three days to clear. Three days of "practicing" with Teddy, and in those three days he got good. I also blew right by my limit of only being sexual with an alpha three times. I couldn't get enough of him or his knot.

The other problem? Feelings and lots of them. Very inconvenient when I knew I had to leave, and when I told myself I wasn't going to fall in love anyway.

"Guess we gotta go back to work, huh?" Teddy said, panting as he lay beside me in his bed.

"Guess so," I replied, my body damp and wrung out like a rag. "What are the chances that everybody *doesn't* automatically know we spent my heat together?"

Teddy grinned up at the ceiling. "Slim to none, but I'm good with that." He walked his fingers over and linked them with mine.

It killed me to do it, but I moved my hand, missing the spark of our physical connection, but wanting more than anything to keep Teddy emotionally safe. "Honey, you deserve better than a one-heat stand."

At that, Teddy glared at me. "Who said this was a one-heat stand?"

The fire in me turned up even higher. There was genuine upset and indignation in Teddy's expression, more than I would have even thought him capable of.

I sat up on one elbow, just enough to be able to take in his whole expression. "Teddy, I didn't mean for things to go this far."

"I did. I want 'em to go farther."

"You want to see me again?"

His angelic face was contracted into a frown. "I didn't take you to my favorite place for no reason. The nature preserve is only for someone special. I would never want a one-heat stand with you. It would never be enough."

My lungs were empty, and I filled them only just enough to get a few words out. "I have to be honest. I only really have one-night stands. Or a few times more, but that's it."

"Change that," Teddy said, like it was as easy as flipping a light switch. Maybe this time, for this alpha, it was.

"I'm gonna have to leave."

"I know. But you're here now. Be here with me now." He reached up to pull me down on top of him like a blanket, holding me close and tender, the way I'd come to love in the past three days. I had to leave, but not right now.

"Okay," I whispered, still short of breath, suddenly asthmatic for the alpha in front of me. I wrapped my arms around his neck, stroking at the hair at the base of his skull. "I want to see you again, too, Teddy." At that point, I had no idea that my birth control had failed, because my body was dead set on carrying this alpha's baby.

All I knew was that I had to see him as much as possible over the next two weeks. There were more dates just as sweet and fun as the nature center. I broke my sex rule, like, one hundred-fold. Jing and I were supposed to go to Rochester, to the one and only Mayo clinic. The original plan was to head up there a week before we were slated to start our rotation and continuing education, because there was no reason not to go and get settled in.

Until now.

Jing whistled when I told her I wanted to stay.

"What?" I grumbled, a flush warming my cheeks.

She snickered. "Nothing, nothing at all."

"If you have something to say, Jing, just spit it out."

Jing was amused. "No need to be testy, Mister Smells-Like-His-Alpha."

I groaned, not able to hold her eye. "I do smell like him, don't I?" Even more than I thought I would. Why was it so strong?

"Stay. I think it's a good thing."

"You do?"

"Chris. You're happy. You're glowing with it. Stay."

I was happy, happier than I'd ever been. "You say glowing like I'm pregnant or something."

Jing raised her eyebrows. "Are you?"

"No! I'm a lot of things, but pregnant is not one of them." That put the image in my head, though. A family with Teddy. Us sharing baby joy, totally in love. I balled my hand into a fist to keep it at my side, to keep from spreading my palm over my navel. For a split second, I wondered if I was pregnant, then I wished I was. Just as fast, I let the thought go. I was in too deep with Teddy and I knew it, but I couldn't help myself.

Jing laid a hand on my shoulder. "Chris. I want you to do whatever you need to in order to be happy. Even if you think it isn't what you should do." What's that supposed to mean? I wanted to ask. The truth was, I was pretty sure I knew.

I stayed the extra week, feeling like I was stealing time, knowing I was breaking my rules, not trusting my feelings, and not totally trusting Teddy, even though Teddy had been nothing but trustworthy.

I stayed with him up until the very last moment I could without missing my flight.

My voice was ragged in his ear as he made me orgasm. A fierce alpha pride burned in his eyes every time he pleased me, every time he pleased his mate. *Easy there, Chris. You've gone way too far with all that.* Still, every time Teddy made love to me and I loved it, my head spun when I thought of a month ago, when I thought I was hopeless, and now somehow I'd stumbled into paradise.

"Don't wanna let you go," Teddy whispered in my ear. I clung to him, shaking. "Babe, are you okay?"

"I'm fine." I closed my eyes when he pulled back to look at me. I didn't look fine. The corners of my eyes were wet.

"You're not fine. I hurt you."

I shook my head emphatically, my eyes still closed. "No, no, no, you didn't hurt me. You never do."

His body relaxed a little, with the relief of knowing he wasn't hurting me. "Tell me what's going on. I just want you to feel good."

"I know." I didn't let the tear roll down. I wasn't a crier. "You do, trust me." A smirk flickered across my lips, and he squeezed me tighter, trying to connect our skin in every place possible. "It's just that I have to leave. You get that right? I have to leave."

The misery in his voice broke me down. "I know, honey."

"I can't stay."

"I know. You have an important job to do."

"I do. I have to save people. I *get* to save people. That takes travel. I have so much already lined up, planned out to the minute details." I stared at the ceiling now. I was trying to convince myself more than Teddy. I wanted him to keep me in his bed forever, bundle me away from the rest of the world and tell them they couldn't have me. I knew better than to be so selfish.

I looked at the blinking clock on his nightstand and cursed. "I'm gonna take a shower, then I gotta go." I got in and got out lightning fast. Back in Teddy's room, I tried to hop into my jeans. I got one pant leg on, but the other wouldn't go and I tipped against the dresser, making the mirror sway. Teddy giggled. My harried expression broke up for a moment to give him a fake scowl. I turned back to finding the clothes I tossed away last night. "I gotta catch my flight, Teddy. I'm already cutting it close." We'd stolen a lot of time. The gig was up, and now I had to pay the piper.

He climbed out of bed and threw on a pair of sweatpants. "Let me drive you to the airport."

"I have to go home for my things, though."

"I know. I'll take you home, too, help you get packed since I distracted you so much."

That made me smile again. I didn't want to fight him, so I relented. "Okay."

I should have fought him. He helped me pack and held my hand all the way to the airport, then helped me carry my bags to the door. Before I got the chance to walk away, he wrapped me up and held me.

"I gotta go, Teddy. I can't miss my flight." I probably could. It was super short and on a small plane, but it was the principle of the whole thing, the symbolism.

"I get it. I've already been stealing time. Is it so wrong for me to want more?" *All of the time,* his eyes said. *Forever.*

The last time I tried that I got burned, bad. My heart wanted me to stay, but I couldn't risk it, not for a three-week fling. *That's not what this is and you know it, Chris,* my heart said. "Teddy, I'm not sure if that's a good idea. I'm gonna be on the road, I'm gonna be busy, I'm gonna be exhausted, I'm gonna be working long, weird hours…"

He nodded, trying to make his smile kind instead of regretful. "I get it. I knew from the beginning that this was all temporary. It was just a silly date from a silly auction, right?"

"No." I grabbed his face, looking into his eyes from a breath away. "This meant the world to me. I don't want you to forget that."

"There's just not enough to go on from here." I didn't answer, and my silence spoke volumes. I wanted there to be. My omega instincts were saying *yes, there is,* saying *don't leave,* asking, *Why can't we try? Isn't it worth it for us to try?* "This isn't goodbye, though. We'll still talk."

My eyes went back and forth, searching his face. I opened my mouth and my guts twisted in knots thinking of saying no. I couldn't. What harm would it do to text every once in a while? "Of course, we will."

"Okay. Let me know as soon as you land." He squeezed me and I squeezed back, and we held on for much too long, until an announcement about my flight came on the loudspeaker.

I muttered a curse. "I gotta go, baby."

"But we'll talk soon," he added quickly. "I need to know you landed safely."

"Text you as soon as I touch down." I wasn't sure if that was a good idea, because I wanted a clean break and everything about this was messy. Everything about this also felt wrong, right down to the depths of my soul. Especially now that we'd been together so many times, had connected body and spirit. I was even beginning to smell like him something serious. I was missing something and I couldn't put my finger on what it was.

I gave Teddy one last kiss, soft and sweet, then I hurried through the automatic doors, which closed behind me with a soft whisper of their gears.

The last thing I heard was him mumble to himself. "You'll see him again soon, Teddy. Real soon."

That couldn't be true, because this was the end. Right?

10

CHRIS

"THIS IS IT," I WHISPERED REVERENTLY. "THE MAYO CLINIC."

"We've made it to the big time, my friend," Jing said. We'd just checked in at the customer service desk right inside the entrance and were waiting for a representative to come fetch us. There were other visiting physicians, so we made conversation with them, and I snuck a few pictures as we waited.

I texted them straight to Teddy. *I'm finally here. My dreams have come true.*

He texted back immediately. *Incredible! I'm so proud of you, baby.* Why did he have to turn my heart into goop?

"Texting Teddy again?" I jumped at Jing's voice in my ear.

I angled my body away from her so she couldn't see my phone screen, even though she was craning her neck, trying to peek. "Who said I was texting Teddy?"

"Those heart eyes, Captain Obvious. You must think I'm pretty dumb not to have noticed you tripping over your own feet to get to the phone every time it so much as beeps, and I know when you're talking to Teddy because you look like you just won the Powerball."

"You're smart, okay, smartie-pants? It's not too late to join the FBI. You'd make the perfect snoop." I felt like I *did* win the Powerball with Teddy. Like he was my hundred-million dollar prize. So why was I still so afraid?

When I left Clearvale, I told myself I'd start to separate myself from him. We had slept together countless times, and by the end of it, I was a wreck, almost crying and everything. I don't cry. *That means something,* my instincts whispered. *That means everything.*

A confident voice projected into the large space, shutting down my internal monologue.

"Welcome, welcome, everyone." A statuesque alpha woman came in, impeccably dressed with shiny black hair and a bright white smile.

I elbowed Jing in her side. "She's incredible. She looks just like you."

"Awwww."

"If you were tall."

"Hey!" She elbowed me back, but we quickly quieted down in order to hear her greeting. She swept us through the halls to a huge meeting room where there was a catered lunch waiting for us. I rushed to get in line, dragging Jing behind me.

Jing laughed as I helped myself to a few too many balsamic-glazed short ribs. "I get that the food is fancy and delicious, but this isn't our first rodeo. Why the rush?"

"I don't know. I'm just so hungry." I popped a piece of braised potato in my mouth, making loud, smacking, yummy noises as I swallowed it down. Now Jing was really looking at me weird. "What? It's good."

"Suuuuuuure, Doc Chalmers." She pushed past me with her

plate. I snuck a couple of quick pictures. I set my plate on the table gently and slid in next to Jing. I snapped another picture of my food and sent it to Teddy. I just couldn't resist.

Doesn't it look amazing? He didn't answer back immediately, and I frowned and put my phone away.

"Stop pouting and mingle," Jing whispered, poking me with her salad fork.

"Ow!" I hissed, even though it didn't hurt.

"He'll get back to you as soon as he can. He has a job, too, you know." I refused to acknowledge she was right, I just stuck my tongue out at her just as I got a tap on my shoulder.

"You're Dr. Chris Chalmers, right?" Asked an older alpha man with a Santa Clause beard.

"That's me," I said, grinning and holding out my hand for a shake.

It was pleasant getting to socialize and network with everyone there, but I was a bit preoccupied with stuffing my face and waiting for Teddy to text me back. *You gotta get ahold of yourself, Chris.* I told myself that, but I practically squealed with delight when, at the end of the luncheon and the introductory presentation, I had a text that read, *Looks yummy! Have some for me, too, handsome!* This separation thing was gonna be tougher than I thought.

Their surgical theater was huge and bright and shiny, with gadgets I'd never seen before. I wanted to touch everything. I wanted to learn everything. I wanted to stay forever. Except for the tugging in my gut, a strange pull almost like gravity, wanting to carry me back to Clearvale. I rubbed my stomach, feeling a little less queasy when I held my hand there. I slipped my hand under my sweater when I thought no one was watching. Even if it was a little cold, my palm on my skin was much more reassuring.

I wish Teddy was here. I shouldn't wish anything. We'd seen each other for all of three weeks. I was out of Clearvale. This time, I refused to break my rules and end up with a hole in my heart, even if it did feel like Teddy filled it. With a little time, I'd get over it. *That's a lie and you know it, Chris.* My entire being still seemed to gravitate back to Clearvale, back to the alpha I loved. *Be quiet, heart. You're not in love and for heaven's sake, no more risks.*

Jing leaned over and whispered in my ear. "So when are we moving in?"

"Right now. Let's go get our luggage. Do you think they'll notice us sleeping in the corner?"

"If they do, I hope they make us work it off. I can't believe this place."

I grabbed her elbow and squeezed. I wasn't proud of acting like a schoolboy, but I was bouncing on my toes, holding myself back from fully jumping up and down. The tour was mind-blowing, and when it was over all I could think about was telling Teddy about it. It just wasn't healthy. My stomach was a little upset, so I rubbed it trying to get it to calm down. Was missing him making me ill?

I had avoided calling him, telling myself that texting was innocent, but you only made a phone call when you meant it. My phone was ringing now. The screen lit up with the contact name "Teddy Bear." Little Delores' voice cycled through my head. "Then you and Teddy can bring me your baby." Why was that sounding more and more like an omen with each day that passed?

"Hey," said the voice on the other end. There was that perfect face, smiling at me in that vulnerable way he had.

I clutched the phone, breathless and helpless. "Hey." There

was a beat of silence. Neither of us knew where to start. *I miss you.* I couldn't say it.

"I miss you." Teddy said it instead. He was always the one doing all the heavy lifting in this not-a-relationship.

I closed my eyes and tried to meet him halfway. "Me, too." It was inadequate, a platitude at best, but it was what I had.

"How's it going up there at one of the premier hospitals in the world?"

Now *that* I could talk about. "It's been incredible. I've never seen anything like it. The facilities, the technology, the research, it's like stepping into the space age or something."

"Sounds impressive. I'd love to see it one day."

Come see me, said my stupid heart. I rubbed my upset stomach and ignored its voice. "It's crazy because Rochester isn't too much different from Clearvale, but the entire city revolves around the hospital. That makes it more expensive than Clearvale, that's for sure." There's something else Rochester doesn't have that Clearvale does. I pushed past that. "My first surgery is tomorrow."

"Nervous, baby?"

I shrugged. "For the procedure itself, no. For the setting, a little bit, as much as I hate to admit it."

"Yeah, you must be feeling some kind of nerves if you're admitting it," he teased.

"Shut up. Where's the 'end call' button?" I teased back, pretending to be searching for it, my finger hovering over the phone screen.

Teddy held out a hand, laughing. "Kidding, I was just kidding. Don't punish me by taking away that beautiful smile when I haven't seen it in so long." There he goes again, melting my heart. "You've got nothing to worry about. The confidence you have is well-earned, and you need it to do what you do. Toot your horn all you want, handsome."

The alpha physician who had originally started us on the tour was calling for everyone's attention.

"I gotta go, Teddy."

He gave me a rueful smile. "Darn it. I'm glad I got to see your face, even if only for a few minutes. When can I talk to you again?"

"Um, not for a few days, I think. We need to do all the last minute prep, then the surgery itself, and the next day I'm sure I'll be wiped out and probably buried in paperwork."

Teddy was disappointed, but he didn't push. "Okay. Best of luck, but you don't need it because you know what you're doing. Shoot me a quick text just to tell me how it went."

"Okay," I found myself saying, even though this was the perfect time to start cutting back on our contact.

"Talk to you soon." He kissed the phone and although I couldn't respond in kind, I "kissed" him, too. I clicked off and went back to my day, reminding myself over and over to enjoy this once-in-a-lifetime experience at the Mayo Clinic.

Apparently, I was obvious with my moping, too. Jing full-on tackled me onto the couch the next night. I didn't even struggle, just fell over in a blob.

"You got it so bad, my friend," Jing said as she sat on my legs. She leaned down and sniffed me. "How do you smell even more like him?"

"I do?"

Jing leaned over me, giving my cheeks a few quick taps, sharp enough to wake me up a little. "Why are you doing this to him? Why are you doing this to yourself?"

"Because it's not gonna work!" I moaned, drawing out the "o."

Jing put her hands on her hips, glaring down at me like a disappointed, scolding mother. "He's not Guy, Chris. He's literally the complete opposite of Guy."

"I know," I moaned, holding my balled fists up to my temple.

"Why are you fighting him? You already smell like him. You reek like sex and pheromones and some other stuff, god only knows what." She waved a hand at me.

I was losing my grip. I ached to be with Teddy, but if he hurt me I'd never recover. "There's too much to overcome."

"Correction. There's a *lot* to overcome. It's not impossible if you want to put the work in, and you and I both know you want to. Teddy would walk a mile over hot coals for you. If you told him what you needed, he'd do it and say 'thank you from the bottom of my farmboy heart.'"

Jing was right about everything, of course. I sniffed myself and she burst out laughing. I smelled different and my body felt a little different since I'd been with Teddy. Being with him was changing me. If it was because he was my mate and the love of my life, shouldn't I want to know?

Jing continued. "People make long-distance relationships work all the time. It just takes extra dedication. You'll just have to text and call each other all the time, which you already do," she held a hand out to indicate my phone in my hand. I quickly stuck it behind my back, like that made any difference. "You'll have to go back to good ol' Clearvale a little more often, or you could come back to Mayo more often and he could meet you here. Awesome for your career and not too far." I tightened my jaw. Jing was coming up with a hell of a lot of good points. "Sure, you'll miss each other like crazy, but when you see each other, you can make up for lost time, if you know what I'm saying." Jing made a little thrusting motion with her hips. I burst out laughing, but I also caught fire, just a little, like a lit match. Every time I'd been with Teddy, he fanned my flames into an inferno with his eagerness to learn, and his unrelenting desire to please me. Over and over and over again.

"Could you stop thinking about boning him for five minutes? Gross." I opened my mouth but nothing came out. "Can't even argue with me, can you?"

"Guess not. I just don't know how to overcome it all, Jing."

She threw up her hands and climbed off me. "You're hopeless. You need to figure your shit out, my friend, before you make a big mistake."

I'd figure out how to make a full break from him sooner or later. Eventually, we'd drift apart or he'd lose interest. That's what happened in even the closest human relationships. It was normal, natural, for people to drift apart. Someone might as well peel my skin off for all the pain it caused me, but I'd enjoy him for a little longer, then I'd end it. Or it would end itself. Either way it would end, and my heart would be broken, but I'd be safe.

So why did it sound like a death sentence?

I said countless times that I would never see Teddy again. I should have known I would eat my words.

"What's for dinner, Jing?" I asked the day after the surgery. We were in the living room of our Airbnb, Jing breezing through from the kitchen toward the front door. The bell rang just then. "Thank god it's Friday. I need this weekend because I'm ready to drop. Please tell me there's a delivery guy standing on the other side of the door."

"Not exactly, but I think this delivery might reenergize you. It'll definitely take care of dinner."

"Huh?" I asked stupidly. My stomach did a flip, sensing what was going on before my brain caught up.

The door swung open and standing in the doorway was none other than Theodore Behrens.

I jumped up immediately. "Teddy?"

He stood just outside the doorframe and stared at the floor, hugging the flowers and chocolates in his arms. "I, uh, I-I had some vacation d-days, th-thought I'd come and, um..." I grabbed onto the arm of the couch, because otherwise I was going down. "Surprise?" He said it like it was a question, like maybe I'd be angry at him for showing up like this without any notice. Oh, no. Oh no, oh no, oh no. The part of me that was trying to resist him was freaking out. The rest of me had never been happier. My alpha knew to come and get me. To get us. *Who the hell is us?*

Teddy's smile faltered a little, since I'd been standing there in silence just staring at him for such a long time. "Uh, I brought flowers? And chocolates?"

I shoved the weird "us" thought out of my mind so I could get my feet moving. I ran at Teddy so fast he had to drop everything in his hands to catch me. I jumped right up on him, wrapping my legs around his waist.

"Baby, baby, baby," he said, his gentle voice muffled by the material of my jacket because I was like a limpet wrapped around his face, "You just don't know how much I've missed you."

I was too overcome to speak. I just held on, trying to squeeze him tighter, touching every part of him that my fingers could reach, from the short hair on his scalp to the skin of his neck, cold from exposure to the Minnesota air, to the muscle of his shoulders, still rock hard even through the layers of his coat.

"I think I ruined your gifts."

"I don't care," I managed. He shifted me a little, and then I remembered what a compromising position we were in, because I was waking up in the front of my pants.

Reluctantly, I let go and put my feet back on the ground. That's where I needed them to be, because him being here had thrown a monkey wrench in everything, and all my doubts about us were dying.

I grabbed his face and kissed him for all he was worth. "I can't believe you're here." I thought I'd never see him again.

"I couldn't stay away," he whispered in my ear. It sent shivers down my spine, which reminded me; first things first.

I fidgeted with excitement. "Where are you staying?"

"At a hotel a few blocks away. Jing said we'd need our own place."

God bless Jing, because I was about to tear my alpha apart and I planned to do it in every room of the place. She didn't need to be around to witness it. As a matter of fact, like a true bro, she wasn't around now. She revealed the surprise, then disappeared. "Truer words were never spoken."

"I thought I'd take you to dinner, maybe, or…?"

"Take me home."

"Home, so we can like…be together?"

I chuckled. He was still as cute and innocent as ever, no matter how I tried to defile him. "Yeah, home so we can like, *be together.*"

Predictably, Teddy blushed. "I didn't want to presume."

"You're not. We both want it. Matter of fact," I yanked him closer by his collar. "If I don't get you in me in the next five minutes I will literally die."

"Thank god. I'm ready to frickin' explode."

He drove like a madman to his hotel and threw his keys to the valet. We tore at each other's clothes in the elevator. It was a good thing for security that we were in Minnesota and had some layers to get through, or they would have gotten quite the show.

We just managed to get the door closed before we were going at it, full-on rutting on the floor two feet inside the room. The bed was eight feet away, but for us that was eight feet too far.

As we collapsed to the floor, me already wet and willing, Teddy stopped me.

"What?" I asked in bewilderment. What could possibly be so important that he had to stop now?

Teddy laid out his coat, open with the back side on the floor, then he laid mine in the same way right under it.

"There," he said, admiring his handiwork. "That floor is hard and cold. Want it to be at least a little more comfortable."

"Why do you have to be so…" perfect. "You're just so you." I grabbed onto him, kissing him as I hauled him down on top of the coats.

"That's a good thing, right?"

"That's a great thing." His sweet nature had me totally captivated. I'd never been taken care of or attended to like this in my life. "Hey." I stopped him with a hand on his chest. I grabbed his chubbed-up manhood through his pants. I tightened my grip, massaging at the head just a bit. Teddy's mouth slipped open and his eyes went glassy. Teddy's eyes were hooded, unfocused, mesmerized. Was it wrong that I loved the power I had over this alpha? That I loved how he was so unashamed about being under my spell? That he trusted me to be this vulnerable? I didn't say any of that. I said, "I'm glad you're here."

"Me, too." I let myself be glad, even though I was terrified of what that meant. I'd sort it all out later. Right now, I was gonna enjoy Teddy.

There was plenty of sex, and I lost count of how many times

over my three-sexual-encounters limit we went. Once again, it was all going out the window, and once again I wanted to let it go. We even got a couple of dates in when we could be bothered to leave the hotel room.

Teddy extended his stay by a couple of days, but all too soon our time was up, and I found myself dizzy from the way my emotions spun around my head, flashes of green, yellow, and red telling me to go, go, go, no, slow down, no stop! Most of all, though, I didn't want to close the door anymore. I wanted to give us a chance.

We laid in bed after a particularly athletic round of sex, me on my back and Teddy's head on my chest, a finger tracing circles on my belly, of all places. "I gotta leave soon, babe."

"I know."

"I wanted to talk to you about something, since you're leaving for Dallas next."

"You remembered I'm going to Dallas next? I only told you that once, a long time ago."

He gave me a rueful smile. "How could I forget when I'm so proud, but Dallas gets to have you instead of me?" Shit. It meant so much for someone I cared about to be proud of me. The "l" word was on the tip of my tongue, but I bit it back. Teddy rested his chin on my chest and gave me that sweet, bashful smile of his. "Maybe it's way too soon to even be talking about this, or maybe it's not right at all, but I really need to get it out."

"Okay, what's up, babe?" I had a guess as to wher this was going, and for the first time, I thought I just might be ready for it.

"What if you came back to visit me?"

I ran my fingers through his hair. "I'd love that. I'm not sure how things would shake out with my schedule, but I'd love to come back and see you." There, I said it. I wanted Teddy, and it felt good to just go with it.

"You like Clearvale, don't you? You said it felt like a second home. What if you stuck around for a while when you had a break in your schedule? What if you…maybe even stayed?"

"Stayed?" I echoed, my muscles getting tense. That was different from what I expected. "You want me to move to Clearvale?"

"Well," he bit his lip, trying to backpedal and move forward at the same time. "It's just that what I feel for you is so strong. I can't just let you walk out of my life. We have something special here, don't you think?"

"Yeah, I do." And I'm just now allowing myself to feel that. "Moving is a big step, though, don't you think?"

"That's true, but I just can't stop thinking about it. What if I helped you get a permanent position at Chance Vieth? Not that you'd need much help, you'd be a shoe-in." Teddy was lit up, excited and energized. He talked faster as he thought out loud. He slowed down and put a hand on his chin, thinking. "I don't know how much you'd be able to travel, though. You might not be doing as many procedures. There might be more administrative work involved." My throat tightened up like someone had put a noose around it. Teddy went on. "You'd need a place to stay, and maybe you'd wanna live with me? I'd love that. You wouldn't have to pay for anything…" My head buzzed with white noise. Just as I opened myself up to the possibility of starting a real relationship, I got hit with the "you make all the sacrifices" talk. The last alpha who talked to me about that was trying to lure me in for the kill. *Teddy's not like that*, my heart said, but how did I know? Panic was rising in me now.

Teddy said, "I know it hasn't been long, but-"

I cut him off. "No, it hasn't been long. Only a month, and you're talking about *me* moving."

"Maybe I shouldn't have said that."

My voice and demeanor hardened the more I thought about it. "Maybe not. You're not offering to move to Philly."

"Chris, I only mentioned you moving to Clearvale because you seem to like it there, that's all."

I sat up then, making Teddy sit up, too. His eyes were wide and hurt, and I hated it, but I'd been down this road and I didn't like where I was headed.

"I just think," Teddy started again, stumbling over his words, "that we have something special here and I just want to keep exploring it. I thought you would want that, too." *I do want that. Just not like this.* My heart raced and my adrenaline rushed. My emotions were going crazy, and I was even more reactive than I normally would have been, more hormonal, but I couldn't figure out why. I stood up out of the bed.

"Honey, please. I didn't mean to upset you," Teddy pleaded, his hands out.

I gathered my clothing, balling the fabric into wads in my shaking hands, trying to make some sense of where to put my arms and legs into them. "Well, you did."

"It's just that it wouldn't be easy for us to be together, but I want to find a way. I want to make an effort. Maybe, if we both made sacrifices, we could make it work."

There it was. Now there was only the red light, blinking like a railroad crossing, the train coming down the track to wipe me out, flashing like a red flag, reminding me of everything that threatened me before.

"Sacrifices. You talk about sacrifices, but the first thing you mention is me making all of them. Like my life and career aren't important."

Teddy followed behind me as I navigated my clothing and put it on, even though I was still gross from post-sex sweat.

"Chris," he said, and it was clear his throat was closing up on him, "That's not what I'm saying. You know I know how important your career is. Don't I tell you all the time?"

I turned on him. "Exactly how many of these sacrifices are *you* going to make?"

"Honey, just tell me what you want me to do. I'm listening. If I knew you'd get this upset, I wouldn't have said anything but I-" He cut himself off. Love me?

A weird surge of hormones and instincts overwhelmed me, and together with the nightmare from my past experiences, thinking straight was impossible. I wanted to run to Teddy, because the feelings of love were so real, and my instinctual need to be protected and doted on by him were heightened in a way I didn't understand.

On the other hand was my fear and my pain, and it won the day.

"One month," I hissed. "Only a month and you're asking me to turn my life upside down."

"No, that's not what I'm asking."

"I told you this was temporary from the very beginning. You keep *pushing* me."

Teddy was near tears. "I thought that's what you wanted. I thought you felt the same about me."

You do feel the same, Chris. Don't do this. I yanked on my coat and stomped into my shoes.

"I don't." Teddy's mouth hung open, his eyes red and wet. Some cruel, broken, ugly part of me liked doing this to him, like this was some sort of twisted revenge. Teddy's heart dropped and shattered, like a piece of delicate crystal swept carelessly onto the floor.

Another part of me was beating its head against the wall, screaming *how could you hurt him like this?*

My mind was made up. It was break his heart, or get mine broken later. "This is the end. No more contact. It's better that way, you'll see." I walked out into the Minnesota chill and shut the door behind me.

For the final time, every though every bone in my body screamed at me not to, I walked away.

11

CHRIS

It didn't take long to realize I'd messed up. Bad. Within days, I was physically sick from missing Teddy. I performed the surgeries in Dallas without a hitch, burying myself in my work, but afterward I collapsed and laid in bed for days on end. My heart was crushed and my zest for life was gone. I alternated between working and moping, dragging myself to the places I absolutely needed to go but nothing more, my whole body slumped and crooked like I was eighty years old.

"It's not too late to call him," Jing kept saying. "Do it now. The longer you wait, the worse it'll be."

I just laid a forearm over my eyes, trying to block out the world. "It's over, Jing, I just need to accept that."

"I just can't with you. If you're dead set on suffering, and making Teddy suffer, so be it, but I'm done with watching it." Even Jing had had enough of my bullshit. What else was there left to do but punish myself and try to stop pining for an alpha half a country away?

It wasn't until the nausea started about a month later, that I got suspicious.

"It can't be," I mumbled, spreading a hand over my middle. It can. It is. The voice in my head said. It would explain everything. My body was going through some changes, and my stomach had been rejecting everything lately. There had been more to the heartbreak of missing Teddy, too. That feeling of needing connection to my alpha, of needing to be protected and looked after, had grown exponentially with the little person inside my womb. I already knew, but I needed to be sure.

After a run to a local drug store and the scariest trip to the bathroom of my life, I clutched the test in my hand.

"What does it say?" Jing asked, her pallor abnormally pale and her fingers twitching nervously. When I told her I needed her and why, like the great friend she was she forgot about how pathetic I was and came to be my rock. I held out the test to her from where I was sitting on the floor with my knees drawn up to my chest. "Eww, that has your pee on it."

That surprised a laugh out of me. "I only peed on the tip, silly. Besides, you and I both know it's sterile."

"Yeah, but it's still pee." Despite her protests, she took the test from my hands. "There are two blue lines here."

"Yep."

"One is a control, to indicate that the test is working properly, the other is a confirmation of the hormones that indicate pregnancy."

"Look at you and your big fancy medical degree."

Jing set the test down on the counter without a sound. She stood next to me, leaned against the wall, and slid down with a loud groan until she was on the cold tile next to me. "So."

I nodded slowly. "So."

"This is a pretty big deal you got going on here."

"I'd say so, yes."

"Got any feelings about it?"

"Plenty of 'em."

"Sorted any out yet?"

"Dunno. Maybe a few."

"Wanna tell me which ones you've got worked out, and maybe get cracking on the others?"

"If you insist."

"I do, in fact, insist."

"Thank god, because I gotta talk to you about this." I slid both hands down my face. "Jing, what in the sam heck am I gonna do with a baby?"

"Excellent question, but I'm not sure how you want me to answer it."

I rested a hand on my belly, now confirmed to have a fetus inside, about eight weeks along if I had to guess. "I didn't know I'd feel this strongly about becoming a dad, but now... I've wanted babies for a while now."

"Not to mention-" Jing started, holding up a finger.

I knew exactly where she was going with that. "This is Teddy's baby."

"You want this baby, and you want this baby with Teddy more than anything, don't you?" It was impossible to feel any movement inside with an embryo the size of a cherry, according to one of those baby websites, but I already just *felt* pregnant. I already felt there was a little human in there, listening to my heartbeat, hanging on what their O-Dad had to say.

"More than anything," I replied, and it was true. Teddy was my mate, my life, my future. "I shouldn't have left him."

"Honey." Jing wrapped an arm around my shoulders and tucked me in tight. "You were gunshy after your past experiences with alphas. I don't blame you for freaking out when he suggested you stay. He might have been a little overeager."

"He was, right?"

"Don't get too excited, Mr. Took It Too Far."

I winced. "I did, didn't I? I didn't need to snap at him like that, to make him feel bad. I messed it all up." I wrapped my arms around my knees, hiding my face in shame, acutely aware of my little passenger. "What if I end up like my O-Dad?"

"No way in hell."

I peeked an eye out at her. "You don't think so?"

"Trust me, you and your O-Dad could not be more different as people. He's negative and sour. You have a great attitude, lots of confidence, and you're full of love, in spite of what your 'dating' track record says. If you were a single O-Dad, you'd still hit it out of the park for this baby. You're not gonna be, though. Teddy's over in Clearvale, hoping and praying you'll call him."

I didn't want to hope for it, the way I left things. "I don't deserve for him to be waiting on me, Jing."

Jing threw up a hand. "Says who? So you made a mistake. Problems can be fixed. If something's broken, it can be pieced back together again. Forgiveness is a thing, you know. I'm willing to bet, that if you explained your feelings to him, he'd understand. He's gone on you, handsome. He wants to be able to forgive you, you just have to believe you deserve a second chance and ask for it. Besides, think of that man as an A-Dad. Swoon."

I allowed myself to picture Teddy doting over me with a big, protruding stomach. Teddy by my side in the delivery room. Teddy gratefully wiping our newborn's butt and putting a new diaper on them.

"Oh, that guy's gonna have the time of his life on diaper duty. He's gonna whistle while he works."

"I can't wait to see that. You gotta go get him, but you gotta do it big. He deserves to know that you mean it."

"Should I show up outside his window with a boombox?"

"Something like it."

"A public declaration of love it is." I slapped my thighs and made to stand up. "Let's get crackin'."

I was back in Clearvale within the next few days, stealing time between surgeries to make the flight. Right up until the moment I came to Teddy's floor I was hoping, praying, begging, pleading that he'd forgive me, that he'd still want me. I carried a good luck charm in my hands; milk-chocolates with a honey center, the symbol of our love.

The hospital was bustling as always, with people hustling back and forth, carts, chairs, and beds rolling around, and the familiar scent of antiseptic in the air.

In spite of all the motion, when I got there the entire nurse's station froze.

One of Teddy's coworkers let out a long breath and let their head drop on the counter, rustling a stack of paper. "Thank god you're here. He's been a mess."

"He has?" I asked in surprise.

Someone else added, "We kept our fingers crossed that the two of you would work everything out. Teddy was so happy when you were together, we couldn't believe it."

"You're not all pissed at me?"

"Teddy never told us what happened. Did you do something to him?"

Dr. Gupta was there. He gently laid a hand on my arm. "Yes, Doctor, what happened with you and Teddy?" He asked softly, not in any way accusatory, which I was thankful for.

I dropped my eyes, clutching the gold box in my hands. "I made a mistake. I want to make it right. That is, if he'll let me."

Dr. Gupta nodded thoughtfully. "I see. I think he'll let you."

"You do?" If Dr. Gupta thought so, I had a shot.

Dr. Gupta stroked his chin. "I'm afraid I can't say I'm one-hundred percent certain." My heart sank. "What I can say is that Teddy is the kindest soul I've ever met. Overflowing with love. The two of you had something special, that was plain for everyone to see. I'm not sure what happened between the two of you, but if it is a mistake that can be forgiven, that can be moved on from, it's well worth it to try and he's the type of person that will give it his all."

"I know," I said softly. "That's what I love about him." There. I said it. I got ready to say it again, to his face.

Dr. Gupta nodded knowingly. "Either way, I think he should hear your explanation and hear your apology, and he can make his decision. I have a good feeling, though. I want to see him happy again. Happy with you."

I nodded and tried to smile. Some hope but no promises, and I understood that. No matter what, I'd try, and I'd give Teddy what he deserved emotionally. "At least I'll be able to say I tried my best."

"I'll go get him."

A few minutes later, Teddy emerged from a patient room in his favorite Space Jam scrubs. "What's going on, Dr. Gupta? Is someone-" He stopped dead when he saw me, a few yards away. His face went on a journey, from shocked to excited to loving to angry and right back to shocked. "Chris. You're here."

I nodded and said, in my quaking voice. "I'm here."

He shook his head, confused, his face clouding with something like bitterness. "But why?"

"I have something I need to tell you." I raised my voice so it filled the already loud hallway. "Excuse me, everybody, excuse me. I have something I need to say."

All the shocked people in the hallway ground to a halt. My skin burned from all the eyes on me. *I asked for their attention, now I got it. Let's do this.* "Thank you all for letting me interrupt your busy day. I won't take long. I just need to say that I came back to Clearvale for that alpha right there." I pointed at Teddy and everybody swiveled their heads to look. Teddy blinked in surprise at all the people looking back at him, many he'd known for years.

"That alpha, for those of you who don't know, is the kindest, most caring, most dedicated, and strongest person I've ever met." Teddy took in a sharp inhale, even more shocked than he was before.

I went on, speaking in turn to every person there. Another nurse with all-blue scrubs. A parent pushing a tween girl in a wheelchair. A custodian with a mop in hand. "He's also the most courageous person I know. He had the courage to be vulnerable with me, to tell me the truth, and to take a chance on me. I did not have that courage, and because I was a coward, I made the biggest mistake of my life." I looked my alpha straight in the eye. "Teddy, when I said I didn't care about you, I was lying to the both of us. The truth is, I'm in love with you." Everyone around us gasped. A bunch of staff at the nurses' station went "aaaaawwwww." There, it was out. Now he knew, and he had a chance to decide what that meant for him.

My throat was clogged with emotion, but I pressed on. "I kept leaving you, and I'm sorry. If you hate me, if you're angry with me, if you never want to see me again, I would understand because I deserve it. But if you could give me another chance," I walked toward him, holding my hands up, pleading with everything left in me, "I want to make sacrifices together. I want to experience the bliss I felt every time I was with you. I want it for as long as you'll have me.

"So I'm putting myself out here for everyone to see so that you know how sorry I am, and how serious I am, not only about making things work with you, but making things wonderful with you. Being with you is truly wonderful. I was a fool to walk away. If you give this fool a shot, I'll never walk away again." I held out the chocolates, and I shut my damn mouth.

Teddy just stared at me. His face kept changing, but it didn't look happy. I wasn't seeing forgiveness. *Oh no. I messed things up too bad. This is all my fault.* I tried, but I failed. The humiliation made it worse. Dozens of people witnessed me shoot my shot and crash and burn. Teddy wasn't accepting my gift, the chocolates I held out to him, both as an olive branch and as a representation of our relationship so far. Now was the time to run, to tuck my tail in between my legs and go find a rock to crawl under, and if I wasn't pregnant, I would prefer to die under there.

I took a step back, shrinking in every dimension. "Okay, I, um, I guess I'll go now." I turned away, keeping my face aimed at the floor so I didn't have to see anyone's face reflecting back at me how pathetic I was.

A hand on my wrist stopped me. Teddy. Would he curse me or tell me off? He would be well within his rights to do it, but I'd crumble like stale bread.

"Wait," he said, his face stony in a way I'd never seen. "You say you love me, that you lied about not caring about me. Why did you say it, then? Why did you hurt me like that?"

"I know it's no excuse," I started, pulling myself together to look him in the eye. I wouldn't have been this terrified in front of a firing squad. "But I've been hurt. I took it out on you. I was wrong. I was scared, too. I wanted to walk away before I got hurt. A lot of good that did me, right?" I held my free arm up, indicating toward the hall at large and all the people watching the show. "Teddy, it was the biggest mistake of my life. I accept your frustration, and I want to earn back your trust. If you still want me, I'll do whatever it takes." My heart stopped beating as I waited for his answer.

Teddy's face softened into something familiar, sweet and soft and loving. "Okay."

"Okay?" I asked incredulously.

Teddy pulled me into him. He took the chocolates. "I love you, too, honey. You have no idea." I gripped his shoulders for dear life. Suddenly, my emotions, that I'd successfully held back all this time, burst out. I started sobbing like a child, in front of dozens of people. I hated crying, and all these people were witnessing it. It didn't matter, because I had my alpha back. I blubbered, my face wet and no doubt red and puffy as a Minnesota winter jacket. People around us cheered, clapped, and offered us congratulations.

Teddy rubbed my back. "Don't cry, baby," he soothed. That made me cry harder. If Teddy was shocked I was crying like this, he didn't let it phase him. Why was he so damn good?

"Why are you being so good about this?" I whimpered.

He chuckled. "Isn't it obvious how open I am for you?"

"I don't deserve it."

"I don't think that's true. Am I mad? Yeah. Am I hurt? Yeah. I can see where I was a little overeager, though, and I'm sorry about that. I'm just new to being in love and I'm so excited about you that I got a little carried away." I squeezed him tighter. "I also could have done better about discussing how we slowly work out changes together, instead of just listing off ways that your life would change. I was just thinking out loud and I shouldn't have started with ideas about what *you* might need to do, because that wasn't fair. I'm guessing you had a reason to freak out, though, and I'm hoping you'll tell me what it is so I can understand you better. Then we can figure out how to move forward."

I pulled back just enough to look at his face. "So you're saying yes? You want to try with me? You want to be with me?"

"Honey, it was always you, from the moment you picked me off that stage."

I cried harder, burying my face in his neck and holding on. It felt good, knowing I was able to trust him, that he was a solid rock I could cling to.

Dr. Gupta appeared next to us. "This was beautiful, Doctor. I'm glad you came back, not just for him, but for you, too. You shouldn't have to live without each other."

I smiled, still clinging to Teddy. "Thanks, Doctor."

"Teddy, I think you should take the rest of the day off. We can cover for you, right everybody?" Everyone behind the nurses' station eagerly agreed.

"Thanks, everybody."

"Get out of here, Teddy," the medical assistant said, shooing him with one hand from where she sat in front of a desktop computer. "Go be in love."

He gave them a silly thumbs up that made me laugh. "Roger that!"

We ran out of the hospital hand-in-hand. We jumped into his car, and once we were inside his home our hands were all over each other.

Then I remembered the other important thing.

"Teddy, wait, wait." His eyes flashed with panic, so I quickly added, "Don't worry, nothing's wrong. I'm so glad you said yes, because there's something else I need to tell you."

He kissed my neck and smiled. "Lay it on me."

"You're gonna be a dad."

He tilted his head like a puppy. "Whaddya mean?"

His cluelessness was adorable, and I couldn't help but laugh, just a little. "Honey, you know what sex is for, right?"

"Well yeah, like, it's fun, and it can bring two people closer together, and it makes babies…" His eyes bugged out and he gasped. "Did we make a baby?"

"According to like, five pregnancy tests, yeah we did."

Teddy was aghast. "How did it work that fast?"

I was really laughing now. "It only takes one time, and we did it *lots* of times. You know this, you're a medical professional."

"I know, but this is *me* we're talking about. I'm late to everything that has to do with reproduction."

"Well, you came in first place here, pal. I should get you a blue ribbon like in 4H. Teddy Behrens, prize-winning cock." Teddy hid his face in my shoulder, embarrassed and giggling. Gratitude radiated in the spots where he touched me. I had my alpha back. "You still haven't told me what you think, or how you feel."

"About what?"

"About me being pregnant."

"Oh. I'm excited, obviously. It happened way sooner than I would have planned, but it was always the plan."

"Me barefoot and pregnant, huh?"

"You pregnant, wherever and however you wanted to be."

I shook my head in wonder. "You make this so easy."

He laughed and kissed my jaw, "I've been dreaming about having a baby with the one I love for the longest time. Besides, I told you, I'm easy for you."

"Teddy, I have to be honest with you about why I acted the way I did. I've been hurt."

Teddy nodded slowly. "I thought that might be the case, before."

"I never let any alphas get close. I had these rules. At least, I had them until I met you, then they all went out the window day one." That got a smile out of him. I cleared my throat and continued. "I had broken a few rules for an alpha I thought I had feelings for, right before you and I met. I let this guy in and he turned into somebody I didn't recognize. He was condescending. He was controlling. He was shallow and self-serving. I'm not sure if he hid it well, or if I just wasn't paying close enough attention. Probably a little of both." I chuckled dryly. "By the time I got to Clearvale, I was running from him and my situation, and the complex my O-dad has given me." I told him the dirty details about my toxic O-Dad and how the lack of approval had affected my self-esteem and my ability to be monogamous. I pressed the heels of my hands into my eyes. "I'm just a mess."

Teddy had a proud little smile on his face when he said, "You're my mess now. Thank you for telling me that. Thank you for coming back for me, for telling me you love me."

"I had no other choice. I just couldn't live without you."

Teddy kissed me, gently but passionately. He backed me into his bedroom, to the edge of his bed. "Sit. Relax. I'm taking care of you tonight." I blinked. It was so similar to what I'd heard before, but everything about the situation was different. Everything about this situation was right.

As my alpha laid me down to make love to me he whispered, "Here's to the first day of our forever."

"To the first day of forever." We marked it with a kiss.

12

———————

TEDDY

"Holy moly." It was the first thing I said when I woke up that morning. Chris had just rolled over, from having his back to me to facing me. Our room was bright with morning sunlight, which might have hurt his eyes. When he was on his back, I noticed a little something. I couldn't help but notice this little something. This *big* something, actually.

"Chris. Chris, are you awake?" I knew he wasn't quite conscious yet, but today I couldn't help but speed the waking process along a little, especially seeing what I saw when I looked down. "Chris," I tried again. He made a little sound but didn't stir. Okay, so no waking up right now. Could I get away with touching him?

I slipped a hand down and spread my palm. I tested with the tips of my fingers; Chris didn't stir. I slowly made contact with more and more of my hand, until my palm was right up against Chris' belly. His big, round belly. Finally, he'd really popped. I enjoyed the convex shape of it, firm in my hand. My baby was in there, and they were growing.

I didn't want to wake Chris, but I was so delighted I didn't know how to wait. I carefully peeled back his pajama shirt to reveal his skin, tight as a drum, his belly button protruding now. Skin-to-skin, I felt the warmth, the connection.

"This is the best thing ever," I whisper-shouted.

Chris cracked an eye open, mumbling sweetly and sleepily, "What are you doing, Teddy Bear?"

"Babe, look at you. You're incredible."

"What?" He looked down. "Where'd that come from?"

"That's what I said! I didn't know it literally happened overnight when you popped. I thought you weren't going to."

"I wasn't sure if I really would, either." Chris was approaching the six-month mark in his pregnancy, and the whole time he hadn't had much of a bump. When he wore baggy clothes or a jacket, you couldn't really tell he was pregnant. That had been a huge disappointment to me as a first-time A-dad. I would love my mate and baby either way, but I'd been hoping for more visual evidence of the pregnancy. Now, I had it.

"I didn't wanna, like, complain, and I didn't wanna rush them or rush you, but…"

Chris laughed at me. "But you wanted to see your baby poking out there."

I rubbed circles over his baby bump, admiring how filled out and round it was now. "Yeah. It's so many things. It's special, it's cool, it's…"

"Hot? You can say hot."

I shook my head in astonishment at just how much of a turn-on it was. "Really flippin' hot, babe." Chris threw his head back against his pillow and laughed. It was a perfect little moment. I took a mental snapshot and committed it to memory.

Getting ourselves set up to become a little family had taken some doing. Chris had to reduce and reschedule many of his future surgeries, much to the understandable chagrin of worried parents, but many were able to plan to come to Clearvale.

I managed to get a schedule that was three twelve-hour shifts, so even though I was a little more tired, I had more opportunities to travel with Chris for long weekends, to watch over and pamper him as the baby grew within him.

We also did lots of things to have fun and bond ourselves as a couple. A few months ago, I went back with him to Philly to meet some friends and do a history scavenger hunt. I also met his O-dad, who I wasn't a fan of, if I was being honest. Luckily, we didn't stay long. Back home, we explored Clearvale and the surrounding towns from top to bottom, and my moms were already madly in love with Chris and treating him as their own. Life wasn't easy, but life was good. We were making it work, and it was worth it.

My phone buzzed and tinkled as my alarm went off. I thumbed at the screen to get it to quiet down, then reached for Chris to help him out of bed.

"Noooooo," he groaned. "Five more minutes."

I couldn't deny him anything, especially not today. "Five more minutes, then we gotta get you in the shower. I can't wait to show you off today. Everybody's gotta see." Chris rolled his eyes, but he was smiling. He loved how proud I was of him, how proud I was that he was mine.

"As long as I get to hit my own personal snooze button, I can live with you parading me around a little."

"Deal. Be back in five minutes." Chris dropped his head down and closed his eyes, dozing contently.

I smiled. Maybe I'd give him more than five minutes.

As soon as we got to work, I "dropped him off" at his office then tore off through the halls looking for my friends and coworkers. On my floor, I found Dr. Gupta at the bustling nurses' station typing away at an iPad, entering in patient notes.

My crocs screeched on the floor as I slid to a stop in front of him, my chest heaving as I tried to catch my breath. "Dr. Gupta, come quick."

Dr. Gupta set his iPad down on the counter with a little *click*, his face creased in alarm. "What's the matter, Teddy?"

"Nothing's the matter. I just need you to come quick."

"Something must be the matter. You're out of breath and acting like it's an emergency. Is it the patient in 234?"

I waved my hands, still trying to breathe. "It's not an emergency. I mean, it is, but it's a good emergency."

"There's no such thing as a good emergency in a hospital, Teddy. Tell me what's going on before you give this old man a heart attack."

"You have to look at Chris."

Dr. Gupta's panic only mounted. "What's wrong with him? Should we have the obstetrician see him?"

"No, no, he's fine. Just come with me, okay?" I gently took his arm and steered him toward the elevator bank.

He walked in quick steps to keep up with me. He held up a finger as the nearest elevator dinged and its gleaming silver doors slid open. "I'm trusting you when you say this is a good emergency."

"Just wait and see."

Chris cracked up when he saw me coming, Dr. Gupta in tow.

"You were serious, weren't you?"

"As a heart attack," I answered. I held out a hand to help him out of his chair. "Your balance must be a little off now."

"That it is." He was a little unsteady standing up from the chair. Dr. Gupta stood there, confused, until he saw how Chris' sweater pulled over his middle.

Dr. Gupta slapped a hand to his forehead. "Oh my goodness! You're pregnant!" He'd already known that for a long time, of course, but things took on a new dimension now.

Chris beamed and cupped his belly, pulling his sweater and white coat back to emphasize the new curve. "I sure am."

Dr. Gupta put his balled up fists on his hips. "This is surely a miracle of life."

"That's how I feel," I said.

"This is surely a miracle of Gupta's doing," he added.

"Thank you, Dr. Gupta," Chris and I said in perfect harmony, giggling because we'd done it so often. It was his favorite thing to remind us of his part in how we got together, and we were more than happy to indulge him.

Dr. Gupta beamed, like a proud father. "You're so very welcome. I can't wait to see what the coming months bring us as the little one makes their appearance." He patted my back. "This was, indeed, the best kind of emergency."

Standing there gave me a chance to calm down from rushing to grab Dr. Gupta. Now that I had my second wind, I gave Chris a kiss on the cheek and I power-walked all the way to the cafeteria on the ground floor, taking the stairs, dodging patients and nurses and carts and beds as I went.

Jing was in her usual corner booth near the window, sipping her coffee and eating her yogurt and croissant.

"Jing! Jing! You gotta come quick!"

She raised an eyebrow. "Before I've finished my coffee? I don't think so," she teased.

"Gosh, Jing, I have something you really gotta see."

"Is it a giant Publisher's Clearing House check with my name on it?"

I laughed. "No, but it feels like I have one with my name on it."

"What exactly does that mean, Nurse Teddy Bear? You're speaking in riddles. Does it have to do with my best friend and your mate?"

When I smiled, it showed all my teeth, a lot of my gums, and none of my eyes. "You bet it does."

"Well, why didn't you just say so?" She drained the coffee in a few neat gulps and stood up, smoothing her hands down her coat and button-down shirt. "Let's go."

"Not you, too," Chris said with a laugh when we showed up a couple of minutes later.

"Me, too," Jing said, walking closer to where Chris was sitting at his desk. "Although I don't know exactly why your mate here decided to come get me. I figured it was baby-related."

"It is." Chris stood up from his office chair again, and Jing immediately noticed what was poking out in front of him.

"You're kidding."

I rocked back on my heels, proud enough to explode. "Nope."

Jing came closer, taking a longer look at Chris' belly. "You've barely been showing for so long, I'd thought we'd never get to see them."

"That's the same thing I thought. Imagine how I felt when I woke up to this." I held out my hand toward my mate.

"Pretty damn lucky, I would think."

"You got that right, sister."

Jing rested both palms on Chris' stomach, leaning close to

speak to the bump. "Look at Auntie Jing's baby! You're doing so good, little one!"

"Can you tell I'm proud?"

Chris shook his head, chuckling. "We can tell, honey."

"Can you blame me?"

"Not at all. I'm not complaining about the attention, either."

"I know you aren't," Jing said, which sent us all into gales of laughter. She held out her arms, ushering us all in for a group hug. "Just when I think things can't get any better, we have moments like this." Chris and I stepped up, and the three of us squeezed each other, resting our foreheads together. "We have to let ourselves get lost in these moments. There's so much in the world that's messed up, it can take you under. We need to grab our happiness with both hands and hold on."

Chris chimed in. "You got that right, sister." So we grabbed each other with both hands, and we held on.

I didn't bother Chris the rest of the day- okay, maybe I brought a couple of other people by, but I did drop in to kiss him goodbye when his workday was over and give his belly a rub.

"Bye, Honey and baby. See you at home." A yawn stretched my mouth open. I looked at my watch. "I better not start in on that. I got a few hours to go yet."

Chris cradled my face in both his hands. "This is why I love you. I never thought you would make sacrifices in your career to help me with mine. I hoped for a supportive alpha, but I expected them to still be unwilling to bend with their own desires, you know?"

I shook my head slowly, enjoying the warmth of his palms on my cheeks. "No, I don't know. I'm not saying any of this has been easy, but I've been happy to do it. For you, for me, for all of us." I laid a hand on his belly.

"That's what I mean." He laid a hand over mine, both of us feeling the baby kick within. "It's like you've been overjoyed to make the adjustments to be my alpha and father to our child."

"Well, duh," I teased like a fifth-grader. "The universe aligned so we could meet, fulfilling every dream I've had for years but thought were impossible for me, and with an omega I *really* should not have been able to get."

Chris chuckled and rolled his eyes like he always did when I said that. "Whatever, flatterer."

"You say that every time, like you're not genuinely incredible."

He pretended to relent. "Fine, fine. I'm incredible. Only if you say so."

I wrapped him up in my arms and stuck my nose into his neck, snuffling in his scent and making him squeal. "That tickles. Speaking of how incredible I am…" He whipped his phone out of his pocket, "Look what I got today."

It was a picture of, of all people, little Delores. I gasped. She stood on a green field in a neon green soccer uniform, hands on her hips and one foot on a soccer ball.

"Is she really?" I asked, gaping at the picture.

"She really is."

"See? You're incredible."

"You're just as incredible for being the nurse practitioner you are."

"Thanks, honey. Now get out of here. You better be in bed when I get home."

"No problem there. Goodnight." He waved and I watched him waddle away, my heart brimming with love.

Because my shifts were so long and Chris needed the rest, we had to wait until the next day to drop in on my moms.

I let myself in and immediately started yelling. "Mama! Ma!

We're here! We dropped by with a big surprise for you."

"My sons have come to visit!" Mama poked her head out of the kitchen, wiping her hands with a soft yellow dish towel. "A surprise? For us?"

"Yeah, come see!" I waved her over and walked Chris deeper into the living room. Ma was in her spot on the couch watching a rerun of a classic baseball game. She twisted around to look over the back of the couch.

"Hey, boys, what brings you-" She stopped mid-sentence. "Well, I'll be. Mama, get in here!"

Mama scooted in, the damp towel thrown over her shoulder, speaking in a singsong voice. "I'm coming, I'm coming, I'm-aaaah!" She screamed and threw up her hands. "Look at my baby!" Both of my moms descended upon my mate, happy as a couple of clams. They hooted and hollered and fussed about his new tummy, and I don't think any of us had ever been so happy. Another one of those special moments to snapshot in my head.

Mama patted Chris' belly gently. "This calls for a big celebration breakfast. I can't have my son and my growing grandchild going hungry. You need to keep up your strength."

Chris held up a hand. "That's okay, Mama, I'm not really hungry." The three of us froze and stared at him. He looked back and forth between the three of us and backtracked. "Oh, um, I mean, I'm starving, bring on the feast!"

"That's more like it," Ma said.

"Smart young man," Mama said. We all laughed as she hustled into the kitchen to cook us up a smorgasbord.

Unfortunately, we didn't get to sit in our happiness very long. We had gotten home from my moms' house about an hour before and were enjoying some much needed downtime cuddled up on the couch.

Chris' phone buzzed with a familiar ringtone; his father.

Looking at the name on the screen, Chris' face became drawn and pale and he seemed to age ten years immediately.

"I'm just gonna go take this really quick," he said, his mouth barely moving from all the tension in his face.

"You don't have to." Every time Chris got off the phone with his O-dad, he was an emotional wreck. It wasn't fair to him that his relationship with his father came at such a high cost, especially when he was pregnant.

"Yes, I do, or he'll get mad."

"And do what, Chris?" I asked gently.

"Just...I have to take this." He untangled himself from my embrace. "Hey, Papa, how are you?"

The words on the other end of the line weren't clear, but the tone was and it wasn't good. "I know, I know." That was Chris' "placating Papa" voice. I hated it.

It was harder to hear him in the kitchen, but it was obvious that things were going south as usual.

I couldn't stand this anymore. I just couldn't take it. I stood up and followed him into the kitchen. Chris rapped nervously on the counter, swaying back and forth, his hand on his lower back as his belly poked out in front of him.

"What's the matter?" I asked.

Chris had folded one arm over his now-protruding belly, practically hugging himself, while the other was holding the phone up to his ear. He looked and smelled distressed, which distressed me because I couldn't stand to see my pregnant mate upset.

"Nothing, it's fine." He tried for a smile as he waved me away, but he was near tears and Chris was not a crier.

"It's not fine, Chris," I pressed. "Tell me what's going on." The voice on the other end got angrier, louder, and I decided I really didn't need all the details. I wasn't a tough guy, and this wasn't easier for me, but I steadied myself and let my righteous anger lead the way.

I firmly took the phone out of Chris' hands. "Yeah, this is Teddy. I wanna know what's going on around here." Chris' mouth dropped open.

There was quiet on the other end of the line. He clearly wasn't expecting this. "I'm having a conversation with my son, not you. Give him the phone back."

"Hell, no. I asked you what's going on, and I expect an answer." Now Chris was really staring. I didn't know who was more shocked, him or me.

"What I speak to my son about is none of your damn business."

"When you're having a conversation with my mate that leaves him stressed out and upset, especially while pregnant, it is my business."

"You listen here-"

He tried to start, but I cut him off.

"If you can't show Chris the respect he deserves, not just as your son but as a person, then I'm going to limit how much contact you can have with him." I was not expecting that to come out of my mouth. The last thing I wanted was confrontation with Chris' dad. I never wanted to be disrespectful, but he was forcing my hand here.

There was a pause on the other end of the phone. I waited, a queasy feeling in my stomach, but sticking to my guns for my mate. I just hoped Chris didn't hate me after this.

"What did you say?"

"I said, that Chris is pregnant and he's my mate, and I'll do whatever it takes to make sure he's happy and healthy, including protect him from you."

"You can't protect him from me, there's nothing to protect him from. I'm his father."

"All the more reason for me to put a stop to this abuse."

"Wha- what? You're out of your mind, accusing me of abusing my own son. I can't be abusing him, I gave him life. He's my child."

"The definition of abuse is to treat someone cruelly or violently regularly and repeatedly. Chris is upset every time he gets off the phone with you because of the cruel and mean things you say to him. He deserves love and support."

Papa was stuttering now. "I do support him. All the time."

"How?"

"I, well, I, I try to help him by giving him advice."

"You browbeat and bully him and ignore all the incredible things he's done with his life. He finally did what you've been on him about and you're still not satisfied, which means that you never cared whether or not he was mated and had a baby, only on taking your anger out on him." Now it was really quiet on the other end of the line. I could cut the tension with a knife. I was sweating bullets but I held my ground, for my omega and for my baby.

"I don't have to put up with this shit, not from him and not from you."

"Then don't."

There was shocked silence on the other end of the line. Chris' dad clearly had never had Chris stand up to him, or anybody stand up to him in Chris' stead. I was nervous, but I had nothing else to say so I held. After another few beats, there was only dead air as the other end of the line went dead.

I blew out a loud, audible breath. That had been painful. How must Chris feel?

Chris dropped his forehead onto my shoulder. "Thank you."

I wrapped my arms around his back, smoothing my palms up and down a few times before encircling him, grabbing hold of one of my wrists. He nuzzled into my neck, scenting me.

I scented him back, my alpha instincts satisfied at the receding of the distress in his scent. "You're not mad at me?" I asked softly.

"I had no idea how much I needed that until you did it. I've never been able to stand up to my dad." He kept his face hidden, murmuring into the fabric of my sweater. "I'm so weak."

"You? Weak? We gotta set the record straight on that." I pulled back and grasped his bicep. "Do I need to tick down the list of your accomplishments, and how confident and down-right cool you are, in spite of your O-Dad's venom? I think we're just always that same little kid with our parents, and it's almost impossible to change, but not impossible. You're strong enough to put some boundaries in place. I'll help you."

He chortled. "I see that!" He tucked his face back into my neck, pressing against me, his stomach pushing into mine. "I can't believe how lucky I am. I have the best alpha in the world."

I smiled in warm, fuzzy contentment. "I'm the lucky one. Wanna lay down?" He nodded. We went to bed at two in the afternoon, curled under fuzzy blankets, me spooning Chris. He backed up into me, fitting as tightly together as possible, and pulled my arm over his waist, curling his hand up in mine. My forearm resting on the side of his bulging belly, where the baby moved and turned every so often.

We'd been asleep for a couple of hours when Chris' phone vibrated. It didn't wake us up the first time, but the second and third times got our attention. Chris' phone rang. Then it rang, and it rang.

Chris looked at the screen and cursed. "Babe, I have to take this."

I eyed his phone suspiciously. Something was up. "What's going on?"

"It's…I gotta go to another room."

"For what?" Chris didn't look at me. He didn't have a good answer. "Is it an emergency?"

"Well, no…" The phone stopped ringing, but a moment later started again.

"If it's not an emergency, I don't see why you need to get out of bed for it. You were comfortable before this asshole started calling, whoever they were. Answer it here." Jeez, didn't I sound like an alpha?

Chris chewed his lip, clearly in distress, but the ringing wouldn't stop so he bit the bullet and tapped the talk key on his screen.

"Why are you calling me?" A voice droned on the other end of the line. I couldn't quite make it out, but it was a male voice, possibly an alpha, for sure a cocky bastard. Jealousy and protectiveness rose up in my chest, thick and viscous. It was an unfamiliar feeling, but I had a lot of unfamiliar feelings when it came to being with Chris and preparing to become a dad.

"Honey, who is that?" My voice came out rougher than I anticipated.

Chris covered the receiver, shaking his head, trying to smile but his eyes looked pinched. "It's nobody. Don't worry about it."

"It's not nobody. They're upsetting you. Obviously, they're not listening when you tell them to leave you alone."

The cocky voice droned on the other end.

"That's my alpha, if you must know," Chris snapped. There was obvious laughter on the other end, followed by a short statement that I didn't hear, but apparently it landed the way the speaker wanted it to. Chris' face twisted into something miserable and beaten-down.

Hell, no. I wasn't gonna stand for that shit.

I held my hand out, curling my fingers toward my palm. "Gimme the phone."

"Teddy," he started.

"Gimme the phone, Chris," I said in a firm voice. He pursed his lips together as he set it in my palm.

"What's going on here?" I said for like the fifth time that day.

"What's going on here is that I was having a private conversation with Chris before you so rudely interrupted."

"I say whether you can or can't talk to him."

The voice chuckled, haughty and amused. "You don't control him. He can speak to me if he likes. I'm an old friend. Guy Guillaume. Maybe you've heard of me."

The asshole that tried to change him and broke his heart. "I know who you are."

That thrilled him. "Do you now? He's told you about me, has he? Told you he blew his chance with me?"

"Obviously not. You're calling him." A snort on the other line. "From what I understand, he kicked you out after you tried to cut him down to prop yourself up."

"Prop myself up? I was trying to lift him up. Show him the finer things in life."

"You were trying to turn him into a trophy, while at the same time undermining his talent and career to make him dependent on you so he'd never be able to leave. You're a talented manipulator, but people only manipulate when they're up to no good, and when they're too cowardly to straight up go for what they want. As a Fortune 500 CEO, I'm surprised you would be so small inside."

Silence on the other end of the line. I struck a nerve and man, did it feel good.

"Big words from someone who's bowing down to an omega. What kind of alpha does that make you? What kind of man?"

I rolled my eyes. His desperate attempts at insults didn't hurt me.

"Let me give you a little advice. A real alpha isn't threatened by his mate's success. A real alpha is confident and secure enough in themselves to know that what matters is their character and how they treat their mate. I don't have to hold Chris back or hold him down to get him to stay with me. He wants me because of who I am inside. You might have a fancy job, title, and lots of money, but none of that could buy you out of your insecurities, could it?"

"You know what?" He hissed. "You two deserve each other. I don't know why I wasted my breath calling."

"Couldn't agree with you more, there, bud. Chris is mated and he's pregnant. By me. He's happy. Don't call him again." I stabbed the red phone button, wishing I could just throw the damn phone. "Asshole." I looked up to see Chris staring at me, mouth hanging open. That made me nervous. "What? You okay, babe?"

"Am I okay? After seeing what I just saw?"

I shrank a little. "I thought I did good."

"Teddy," he threw up his arms. "You were better than good! You blew right on past good! Theodore Behrens, you've never been sexier than you are right now."

"I haven't?"

"No, you haven't, which is why I'm not okay."

"What do you mean?"

Chris grabbed my manhood through my pajama pants, making me hiss with sudden arousal pumping blood through my veins down to the spot he touched. "I won't be okay until I get that knot in me."

"Okay," I squeaked.

"Okay," he repeated, giving me his sexy Chris grin. Somehow, even as pregnant as he was, he jumped me.

After an athletic lovemaking session, I changed the sheets on the bed so now we were swimming in a sea of navy blue. I tucked back in behind Chris again, spreading a palm over his belly.

"I'm ready for nap number two," he murmured.

"Me, too."

"The world feels so much safer for me now." He kissed my arm. "Thanks, honey."

"It's my duty and my pleasure as your alpha."

He laid a hand over the one stroking his belly. "We appreciate it." That was all I needed to feel happy and complete. "I can't wait to meet our little person."

"Me, too. They're gonna be our world."

"Their birthday's right around the corner." Chris said in an excited whisper.

Little did we know, it was.

13

TEDDY

"You like that, baby?" I whispered into the dark, my voice in Chris' ear.

"Yes, I like it, honey. Don't stop." I slid out almost all the way and pushed into him again, achingly slow. "Yes, honey," Chris said again. Even in the evening gloom, it was clear how white his knuckles were from how hard he clutched the edge of the kitchen counter. I spread him a little, just barely able to see myself sliding in and out, his wetness glinting on my shaft in the watery moonlight. I thrust more firmly this time, unable to stop my hips from snapping forward with a little more force, but careful because his full-term belly was huge and I sure as hell wasn't gonna ram my baby into the cabinetry.

"How do you expect me to last when you look like this? When you feel like this?"

Chris chuckled, smug as hell. "You want to please me. You'll last." I leaned over his back and kissed his shoulder. I rolled my hips slowly, getting a long groan out of him. I lived to give him pleasure, and I never stopped until he'd gotten enough. "You're right, like always."

"I know," he said, chuckling but biting off the words as he arched his back a little more and pushed back against me. "Can you go fast for me, please, honey?"

"Think it'll be better if we work up to it."

"I know, but-" I rolled my hips slowly again, cutting the sentence off, getting a moan out of him. "You like to torture me, don't you?"

"Like this? You betcha, I do." I said that just to get a laugh out of him, and I did. I sped up just a little, gripping his shoulders where they met his neck, pulling him back as I thrust forward, the way I knew he liked. I'd made a study of pleasing Dr. Chris Chalmers.

He responded as deliciously as always, throwing his head back, pushing his ass up, making those sweet noises of carnal pleasure.

He lifted one bare foot, his toes curling with pleasure.

He wasn't getting his leg up very high, though, not with his full-term belly as big as it was now.

"Hey look, I got you barefoot and pregnant in the kitchen."

"You're not funny at all," Chris lied, laughing until I angled downward a little, hitting his prostate at just the right angle. "Right there, Teddy. Right there, right there."

"By golly, I'll keep it right there."

He laughed and moaned at the same time. "Can you not? I'm trying to concentrate here."

"Ope, Jeez Louise, didn't mean to throw you off there, pal."

"I can't stand you," he lied again, still somewhere between laughing and moaning. He pushed his ass back on me hard, making me take a step back, almost taking me over the edge. My knot swelled as he bent over at the waist. He folded his arms on the counter and rested his forehead on them, his heavy belly, full with my baby, pointing toward the floor.

"Ooh, ooh, ooh!" He moaned as I picked up the pace, getting louder and louder. I moaned, too. Each thrust into my mate was heaven, and I just couldn't keep the sound in. Everybody should hear about it.

It wasn't long before we both came, my knot thick and stuck deep in my mate. Heaven, pure heaven.

Chris let his forehead drop onto the counter with a slight *thunk*, running his fingers through his hair.

"You okay, honey?"

He wiggled his hips back and forth on my knot a little, taking me the tiniest bit deeper, a laugh in his voice when he made me shout. "Never better."

"Wanna waddle our way over to the couch?"

He clenched down on me. "In a minute, maybe."

"Okay," I squeaked. "Just let me know."

Luckily, my knot was down in about fifteen minutes, so I reluctantly slipped out of my mate and got him cleaned up, which was easy since we were already in the kitchen.

"Now I'm ready for the couch," Chris said with a laugh.

The problem was, as soon as we got settled in, he was unsettled. He squirmed and readjusted next to me, over and over as the Sportscenter countdown droned on the tv.

I was on high alert. "What's the matter, baby?"

Chris shifted again, a sour, irritated frown on his face. "I'm kinda tired, but I can't sit still. I have to get up, have to move."

Could it be? "Think you might be having the baby?"

Chris was strangely casual about it when he answered, "Probably, yeah. Nothing hurts. Nothing's, like, squeezing. I just can't sit still."

"Just make sure you let me know if anything starts hurting, and definitely let me know if anything starts squeezing."

"I will, handsome. For now I need to, I don't know, do a couple of laps or something." He pushed himself to his feet with a groan.

I moved to do the same. "I don't know about that."

Chris leaned on my shoulder and pushed me back down with a gentle smile. "Just walking, okay?"

I still eyed him wearily. "Right where you can see me," he added with an amused grin.

"Suppose that's alright, then."

"Don't worry. It'll help me shake off some nervous energy. If I am about to have the baby, it'll help."

"I'll allow it," I replied, only half-joking as I tried not to freak out about *possibly having a baby today*. Chris just snorted at me being in protective alpha mode and started pacing the lower level of the house.

He went from the living room to the kitchen, through the dining room. His footsteps creaked on the floor as he cut through, my hackles rising because I couldn't see him. He cut through the bathroom, which had two doors for access from either side, then he was back in the living room and I relaxed again. Sort of.

After a few more laps I was up, following behind him.

"What are you doing?" He said with a laugh.

"What's it look like?" I grunted. Judging by his changing scent, there was some *activity*. Were we about to have a baby? "I gotta be your watchdog."

Chris grabbed both my cheeks and pinched, gently twisting my face back and forth. "Awww, Teddy Bear. Look at you getting all grumpy when you're protective."

"Can't help it. You smell different."

"I bet I do. I'm pretty sure it's time. I got some squeezing going on." *Code red. We're having a baby.* Chris smoothed his hands down my cheeks; the whites of my eyes were showing so it was obvious I was freaking out. "Don't panic. I'm fine. We're not in danger of them shooting out right this second."

"How do you know?"

He shrugged. "I don't know. I just *know*."

"Okay." I cupped his belly in both hands. "I trust you."

"Wanna call your folks then watch some college ball?"

"'Kay." I steadied my shaking hands and followed him to the couch.

A minute later, my phone screen lit up as it rung my Mama's line.

"Yello?" She said in her thick accent.

I fumbled the phone in my nervousness. "Hey, Mama, where's Ma? Can you call her over, get her on FaceTime?"

Mama immediately went stiff. "What's going on, son? Is it time? Maaaaaa!" She hollered over her shoulder. "Get down here! Teddy and Chris are on the phone, I think it's baby time!"

"Baby time?" Came Ma's voice from the living room, definitely sitting in her spot on the couch.

"Baby time," Chris replied. "There's squeezing."

"Oh my god, he's having contractions. Ma, get in here!" Mama hollered. Ma appeared immediately, crowding in close, her wide eyes taking up too much of the phone screen.

"You mean we're gonna be grandmas today? Well, I'll be." She crossed her thick arms, and sat back from the phone so we could see her upper half, looking proud and satisfied, the way she did after a job well done.

"This is the best day of my life," Mama gushed, wringing her hands, vibrating with joy.

I gasped, faking indignation. "I thought the day I was born was the best day of your life!"

"Second best, son." Ma said with a chuckle. "We were only in it for the grandkids."

"And now I've served my purpose?" I joked.

"Sure have," Mama added. Then she broke down crying. "My son and his mate are having a baby." She looked back at the phone screen, wiping her tears with the back of her hand. "Seriously, Teddy, we're just so excited and proud of you. We couldn't ask for a greater gift. Our wonderful son found a wonderful mate and has a happy life."

Ma held up a hand. "Don't get us wrong, son. We knew you were doing just fine on your own. You made us proud with the way you've lived your life, the man you've become. We were just looking forward to seeing it enhanced like this," She held out a hand toward us, "because we just couldn't wait to see you in love. We were a little pushy because we know how special you are, and now your time has come."

Chris wasn't a crier, but I was. I wiped away a few tears of my own, pressing my fingertips into the corners of my eyes. "You guys have no idea how much that means to me. To us."

Chris grabbed my chin and waggled my head gently. "I'm grateful you made this guy just for me, and that I get to have you both as moms. I hope you won't mind coming over and changing a few diapers here and there."

"You kiddin'?" Ma scoffed. "I'll have that little bundle wrapped up faster than one of those Chipotle burritos."

Chris laughed. "We're gonna hold you to that."

"You do that. Ope," Ma said when she saw Chris grimace in discomfort. "Get goin' now, and keep us posted on your progress. We're gonna be at the hospital the second you tell us go."

"Okay. Love you." We said our "I love you's" and goodbyes and clicked off the line.

We were floating after the happy call with my moms, but we remembered something at the same time. We looked at each other, and neither of us spoke. Chris' face was drawn, and it killed me because he should feel nothing but joy and be totally stress-free on the day he brought our child into the world.

"Want me to call him?" I asked carefully.

Chris shrugged a shoulder, going for casual but missing by a mile. "Sure. I don't care."

"Okay, I'm gonna call him. If you don't want me to, just tell me to stop." I used Chris' phone so his dad would know who was calling, since I barely knew the man.

I reached over to the coffee table for it. I raised it up to my ear, slowly. Chris didn't object. He was silent, but the tension was thick in the air, and the slightly acrid notes of stress and fear peppered his scent.

I dialed the number. Chris glared down at the coffee table, his hands folded in his lap and his eyebrows furrowed, looking like he was trying to do advanced calculus. He didn't tell me to hang up.

The phone rang and rang and rang, and went on ringing. The sound of Chris' heartbreak got louder with every ring.

"You have reached the voice mailbox of..." The answering service listed the number. I pushed down the anger and frustration on Chris' behalf. Nothing could ruin this day for us, nothing.

"Hey, how's it goin'?" I said in my most affable Minnesotan accent. "Chris and I thought you'd wanna know that we're having the baby today. That's to say, they'll be born today, if they're not stubborn. Congrats, grandpa. Take care." I tapped the red button. That was that.

I wrapped an arm around Chris' shoulders and pulled him close. His head dropped onto my shoulder like he was tired of holding it up. He wouldn't cry, but he was miserable.

"Listen, babe. Scratch college ball. We're gonna pack up, then we're gonna watch ourselves some Golden Girls, we're gonna laugh and cuddle and get ready for the best day of our lives. Then we're gonna go to the hospital, and I'm gonna be right there with you when we meet the newest member of our family. Nothing can take away from this day. Okay?"

"Okay." Chris gave me a small smile, one that was hopeful and excited.

"Okay."

I called the hospital and gathered everything we'd need for our little "trip," then settled in with Chris to watch Sophia, Blanche, Dorothy, and Rose. We only made it partway through season one by the time the contractions were close enough for us to go to the hospital.

The new Omega and Baby wing was beautiful, equipped with the latest technology, and full of comfort items for brand-new parents. I was proud that we, well, Chris, had contributed to this being built, and that our baby would be one of the first born here. Check in was quick and easy because they all knew us. By the time we got to our room, hospital staff were already dropping by to say hello and wish us luck.

The room felt more like a sitting room than the hospital. Instead of harsh fluorescent lighting and stark white walls, there was soft pink paint and warm imitation sunlight.

As we got settled in, Chris started asking lots of questions of the nurses.

"When was the room sanitized? Where are the records? How about the instruments?" It took me a second to realize that, now that we were here and he was in some pain, my normally fearless and confident mate was afraid.

I kissed his temple. "Don't worry, sweetheart. I know there are some unfamiliar faces, but I know everybody or I know their boss." That got a laugh out of Chris. "I'm right here with you, and we're getting the best care, surrounded by people we can trust. Should anything go wrong, and that's only a small possibility, we're in the best place we can be. I'm with you the whole way. Don't ever forget that."

He nodded and squeezed my hand. "Okay."

Everyone was very patient and understanding, and explained things to him to his satisfaction.

One of the unfamiliar nurses, probably a new hire just for the wing, was very warm when she said, "They let us know that you were a very important patient here at Willow Green, Dr. Chalmers. We're glad to have you, and glad you've come to help us save so many lives. It's our honor to help you deliver today."

"Oh." His eyes were shiny. "Thank you. That means a lot." The stiffness leaked out of his muscles, and he relaxed onto the bed.

"See, honey? They've got everything under control. Willow Green is the best, or else you wouldn't be here, right?"

"Right."

"Wanna walk around? You can ask lots of questions and be as bossy as you want." That got a laugh out of him. I held my hand out and he took it. "Let's have a baby."

"Okay."

We walked and talked for a little while, pointing out the architecture of the new wing, admiring the artwork, chatting with other new parents. When we made it back to our room, there was a faint buzzing.

"Oh," Chris said, "forgot my phone." He rustled around in his bag. When he came up with it and looked at the screen, his face dropped.

I crossed the room to stand next to him. "What is it?"

He just held the phone out. The screen said "Papa." I was stuck for a second. I didn't expect him to call back.

"Want me to answer it?" He nodded.

"Yello," I said, just like my parents. There was hesitation on the other end. "This is Teddy."

"Oh," said the voice on the other end, already sounding much more humble than the last time we spoke. "Chris is having the baby today?"

"Yes, indeed." I tried for keeping things light. "We're checked in at the hospital and everything looks good so far."

"That's good. That's great." More silence. "Can I talk to him?"

"That depends. You'll need to change *how* you talk to him, and it all hinges on if he even wants to talk to you." Chris gave me a little smile. It wasn't easy for somebody like me to draw these sorts of boundaries. I was a peacekeeper, somebody who didn't like to argue, but whereas I could sometimes be a doormat for myself, I was happy to be a fortress for my mate.

A long sigh on the other end. "I'll do better today. I won't be so…me. I swear."

I looked up at Chris. "Says he won't be so 'him' today. Whaddya think?"

Chris snorted, skeptical. He pressed his lips together, though, and the bottom one trembled. I covered the receiver with my palm as best as I could. "It's okay if you want your Papa today. If he messes up, the walls go back up."

Chris nodded and took the phone from me. "Hey, Papa. How are you?" A pause as the answer came. "I'm okay. Yeah, it hurts. Crazy that it's only gonna get worse." He chuckled. "Yeah, you can see 'em." Chris tapped a button on his phone to switch to a video call. He extended his arm and held the phone out as far as he could. He cupped his belly, pulling his robe in to show the size of his belly. "See?"

"Look at you," his O-dad said, in the softest voice I ever heard from him. "I'm sorry I missed that. I don't wanna miss anything else." He paused for a moment, seeming to gather himself. "Y'know, I used to get on you for not having this. That wasn't right, because you were doing real good for yourself. Real good. Guess all that wasn't about you, it was just the way I felt about me. Y'know?" Chris kept a mostly straight face, but I knew how much just that simple admission meant to him. "Call me when they're born so I can have a look at 'em?"

Chris cleared his throat. "Yeah, yeah, we'll do that."

"Okay. Talk soon."

"Bye." Chris dropped his arm to his side, the phone dangling in his hand. I didn't say anything, just held him. Chris wasn't a crier, but I was pretty sure I felt a little dampness through my shirt on my shoulder. Today was a good day for crying, I figured.

"You okay, baby?" I asked as I pulled back.

He was smiling. "I'm good. Really good. Ready to have this baby."

In the next few hours, he went from walking and talking to groaning and laying on the bed. My moms appeared, bustling with excitement and settling in with us for the birth.

They weren't the only visitors we had. Word had spread that we were here, and while we were happy to see Jing and Dr. Gupta and a couple of other people, we also got a bunch of other curious staff members. People just kept dropping in. Was it possible to interrupt having a baby?

"No one else comes in until we say so. Baby gets born, we

get settled, then Chris decides who, when, and if he wants to see anybody at all." The tone of my voice surprised me more than anybody, but this was my omega, deep into active labor, possibly moments from delivering my first child. If now wasn't the time to get kinda tough, what was?

Chris blew out a breath between his lips, body relaxing. "Thanks, Teddy Bear, my honey-covered chocolate."

His relief was obvious, and that satisfied me, made everything worth it. Chris' labor intensified. The doctor announced he was moving into second stage labor.

"The pushing part." I said.

"The pushing part," Chris and the doctor said at the same time. Chris groaned in pain. Then he doubled over. "They're coming out," he ground out, moving into a crouch. He faced the headboard, clinging with both hands, his back to the room. His back muscles and the lines of his shoulders were tense, completely rigid with pain and exertion. The seconds seemed to tick by much slower, as we all watched for the first sign of new life entering the world.

Chris twisted left to right, big belly swaying as he pushed, his voice starting with a grunt but ending in a long groan. He went from kneeling on one knee to the other, his sway slowing a little, his body dipping as he gave it a hard push, along with a loud groan.

"You're doing so good, honey." I brushed his sweaty ridge of hair off his forehead. He nodded, acknowledging my praise, doubling down on his effort. He twisted left, away from me, then slowly back to the right, a shout ripping itself from his throat. "They're coming. Teddy, they're coming out right now."

"Don't worry, we've got them."

"I'll catch your little one," the doctor assured him. "It wouldn't hurt them to land on the bed from this height. Everything's safe, but I'll catch them all the same." Chris swallowed another groan as he twisted left again, pushing, the cords in his neck standing out as his body worked itself to the limit. "There we are. They've got a little bit of hair."

"They do?" I laid one hand on Chris', which he clutched hard, crushing my fingers against the headboard. The other I laid on his thigh, taut and straining, leaning over to get a look at my new baby. The doctor was intently focused, his hands positioned to guide the baby out. I couldn't see anything until Chris dropped his forehead onto my hand, twisted again and let out a yell.

There. Just beyond the curve of his buttock, the top of the baby's head, not much bigger than a softball. And yes, there was a small amount of dark hair plastered down against the point at the top of their head.

"Amazing." Chris didn't seem to agree, at least not the way it felt. "They're beautiful, Chris. You made a perfect baby." There was only a small part of them in view, but it was obvious that that was one perfect baby. "Keep going, baby. Keep going, keep going. You got this." Chris grunted, groaned, and strained, and gradually more of the baby's head came into view. From there, Chris took a break, panting hard, his eyes glassy and pinched in the corners.

I leaned my forehead against his for a moment, his hairline soaked with sweat. "Almost. You're so close."

"One more push should do it, Chris."

"C'mon, honey. Give it one more, okay?"

Chris nodded fast, his skin against mine. He gripped my hand so hard my joints popped. He let out a loud long yell as he gave it one more big push. I lifted my head again to watch a miracle occur.

"Here he comes," the doctor said brightly. The next thing I

knew, the baby was in his hands, bloody and gross with the umbilical cord attached to his belly, his thin little limbs tucked up, fingers and toes flexing.

My whole world shifted in an instant. One minute he wasn't there, the next he was, and everything had changed. My brain was consumed by a sort of quiet static, and for a moment I couldn't hear anything. When I came back online, there were tiny chirping sounds coming from the foot of the bed, where the doctor wiped at a tiny little body with a white cloth. My baby, my child. The one I wanted for so long.

Chris lowered his knees to the bed, panting, clinging to the headboard. He dropped his forehead onto his forearm, his body melting as he turned into an exhausted pile of jellied limbs.

"You did it, Chris. We have our baby." I stroked the back of his neck, soaked in sweat, his short hair plastered to his skin. Chris let out a long, slow breath, acknowledging my words but still unable to speak.

"Your baby has male equipment," the doctor said with a chuckle.

"Amazing," I whispered. A boy, unless he determined later that wasn't his gender identity. I wanted to get better about that stuff. I had plans on accepting this kid no matter who he was.

I stroked Chris' hand, still clutching the headboard. "Want to turn over, lay down? The doc's getting him cleaned up, then you can hold him." He nodded, and I helped turn him over and gingerly lay him on his back. He hissed in pain, but the second he was settled he croaked, "Hey doc, hand him over."

"You got it, doc. He's a great looking kid."

"Obviously," Chris said with a chuckle, his voice raspy from shouting. The slightly bewildered baby was lowered onto Chris's chest, and Chris let out a long sigh of relief, his expression both blissful and exhausted. He marveled at our little person, tucking a finger into his palm, watching impossibly tiny pink fingers curl around it. The baby didn't so much cry as make soft little chirrups like a bird. It punched me right in the heart how new and vulnerable he was, and how I'd kill and die for him in an instant.

Chris readjusted our son so he could nurse, and the little guy didn't waste any time getting down to business.

"Wow, look at him go," I said, proud as a peacock. What a weird thing to be proud of. Was this what parenting would be like? We just watched for a long silent moment, soaking it all in.

Chris broke the silence. "What do you wanna name him?"

"We remembered everything but a name, huh?"

"To be fair, we've been handling a lot of business and a lot of drama."

"A lot," he agreed, closing his eyes as the baby ate, quiet and content. "I think he looks like a junior."

"Chris Junior? Maybe CJ? That sounds nice."

Chris chuckled but didn't open his eyes. "I meant Teddy Junior. TJ, I guess."

Just when I thought I couldn't get any happier. I did a little jig with my shoulders. "Really? Are you sure?"

Chris rolled his head over to look at me, opening his eyes. "Teddy, you're a gift to this earth and the best damn thing that ever happened to me." He looked down at the feeding baby. "He's already a special little potato, but if our baby carried your name, it would mark him as somebody doubly special. Don't you?"

Time for me to stutter again. "I, well, maybe-"

Chris cut me off, reaching up with a wobbling hand to pull me down for a kiss. It was sweet, it was gentle, it was passion-ate, it was everything I had all but given up on ever getting. Look at me now.

Since I was already down there, I gave the baby a soft kiss, just the slightest brush of lips over his still-damp wisps of hair.

"I'm so proud of you. I'm so proud of the little person we made." Chris snorted. "Well, I helped make him. A little."

"The fun parts."

"I can't wait to see what's next for us." In my arms, our son, my junior, yawned for the first time. It cracked my heart in two, and I knew I'd do any and everything for this little being in my arms. "Whatever's next, I know it'll be great. Bring it on."

EPILOGUE

Chris

I WIPED MY FOREHEAD WITH THE BACK OF MY WRIST AS I PUT THE final stitch into the patient's little chest. I wiped away the last of the blood with a piece of sterile gauze.

"Done," I whispered. My techs stepped in to take over.

"Vitals look great, Doctor." The smile was plain on Jing's face even behind the blue mask. Her eyes crinkled with joy. "Beautiful work. Let's get this little guy into recovery and get his anesthesia reversed."

Everyone in the room let out a series of soft whoops and claps. I nodded, trying to hide the way my eyes teared at the celebration for my first surgery back from paternity leave.

"Thanks everyone. I just want to see this little angel living a healthy life. Couldn't have done it without you."

Jing patted me on the shoulder. "Welcome back, Dr. Chalmers."

I ignored the dampness in my eyes for now. "I was afraid I lost my touch, you know? Afraid I forgot what I was doing and I was gonna botch saving a child's life."

"But?" She asked, eyebrows raised.

"It was just like riding a bike, thank god. I slipped right back into Surgery Mind and my hands went through with everything from muscle memory. Another day of living my dream. Well, part of it."

"I bet the other two parts can't wait to see you."

"And that's why I gotta go. Not even a full day and I miss them like crazy."

"I'll make sure to tell the parents what a bang-up job you did with their son. Get out of here, family man."

"Thanks, Jing. So glad you're my partner in crime." I dropped a masked kiss on her cheek before taking my leave.

I left the surgical suite exhausted, but ready to see my mate and my baby. In the on-call room, I practically ripped my scrubs off then took a quick shower. The warm water was soothing and almost put me to sleep. A half-day surgery on top of having an infant was a killer. If I thought I wasn't getting sleep before, pretty soon I'd forget the definition of the word. It didn't matter, because saving my patients filled me with joy. Having a mate and precious baby filled me with even more joy, which I never would have thought possible. I had it all. I smiled under the shower spray pelting my face.

When I came out, clean, slightly rejuvenated, and freshly dressed, both Teddys were at the main desk in the pediatric wing, surrounded by hospital staff and patients with googly eyes for my baby. *Can't blame 'em, he's adorable.*

Junior lived up to his name. He was shy and never quite sure of people at first, but he was also just as honey-sweet as his A-dad, so when Dr. Gupta pulled a funny face at him, he got a hint of a smile.

"Awwwww!" The whole crowd said. Teddy Sr. bounced our baby in the crook of his elbow, his eyes soft with pride as Dr. Gupta pulled the face again and Junior smiled, then let out one little "A-heh" laugh. What a vision they were.

I ripped my phone out of my pocket and snuck a few pictures, hoping they weren't blurry because I wasn't slowing down. I had to get to my family.

My approaching footsteps were loud on the floor. I moved so fast down the wide, bustling hallway my crocs made a *creak* sound as I got close to them.

Teddy looked up, his face transforming into a look of pure love when he realized it was me. He still smiled with his whole body, happier to see me than I felt like I deserved sometimes.

"Honey, you're done! Look, Junior, it's your hero Daddy!" Teddy took Junior's little hand, no bigger than a half-dollar, and waved it at me. "Say, 'hi, Daddy, who's life did you save today? Are you coming to be Super Dad now?'" He also heaped me with more admiration than I thought I deserved. Call me selfish, but accepting it, basking in it, it made me feel important. Made me feel seen.

"There he is, the man of the hour!" Dr. Gupta held his arms up, announcing my presence like I was a celebrity. A few of the nurses and medical assistants asked eagerly how everything went. They all loved their patients dearly and were on pins and needles while they were in surgery, in the same way family and friends would be.

"It was wonderful. The patient did great, and thankfully, I haven't skipped a beat."

Junior wriggled a little in Chris' arms, getting excited at the sound of my voice. Chris rocked him a little, patting his butt. "Or maybe being an O-Dad made you even more powerful. Strong enough to take over the galaxy."

"You always stroke my ego, babe."

"I like stroking you any way I can."

"Ahem," Dr. Gupta said, loving the way Teddy blushed when he realized how that sounded.

"What?" I asked, smug as hell. "It's true, otherwise we wouldn't have this guy." I held a hand out to point at Junior, who squirmed harder and let out a little whimper. His little sounds of distress always tugged at my O-Dad heartstrings. It was crazy how intense your feelings of love and protectiveness were toward your child.

"Better hand him over. We're both going through withdrawals." I made the little "gimme" gesture with my hands palm-up, curling my fingers back and forth quickly.

I very carefully scooped a hand under Junior's head, still surprisingly small even at four months old, and lifted his little butt with the other. Teddy tilted his arms, angling his body so I'd have an easier time, both of us now used to the shuffle it took to pass our child back and forth to each other. Little things like that were so special, in a way I never expected them to be. Being parents had made us closer, bonded us even further. Being a little family now wasn't easy, but it was well worth it for all the magical moments sprinkled throughout the average day.

Dr. Gupta beamed at the three of us, wagging a finger like a proud godfather. "What did I say, Teddy? Aren't you glad I talked you into going to that bachelor auction? Can you imagine where you'd be otherwise? No Chris, and no baby."

Teddy literally shuddered. "I can't hear about that, Doctor. I won't accept my world any other way."

"Remember when I teased you specifically about Dr. Chalmers? You were skeptical, but even then I knew. Miracles. Just like I said."

Teddy nodded and echoed him, stroking my cheek, then Junior's. "Miracles, just like you said."

Dr. Gupta leaned an elbow on the counter of the nurse's station, looking very smug himself. "I'm so happy. Not just for you, but because I can remind you at any time that this was all my idea."

Teddy rolled his eyes playfully. "I'll never hear the end of this, will I?"

"Indeed not," Dr. Gupta said with a sharp, satisfied head-shake.

"If that's the only price I have to pay, it's beyond worth it."

Dr. Gupta brought his hands together with a *clap*. "Now, when will my wedding invitation arrive in the mail? I've been looking for some time and I have yet to see it."

Teddy and I exchanged a look, eyebrows raised. I was caught off guard, but Teddy looked terrified. Did I want to marry my alpha? Damn right, I did. There was no need for pressure, though. We'd discussed it quite a bit, we knew we both wanted it, but with the baby so young we weren't rushing into anything.

I turned a big smile on Dr. Gupta, one of those polite "thank you, but please don't pry" smiles. "Doc, if and when we decide to get married, you'll be the first to get an invitation."

Dr. Gupta looked at Teddy with a twinkle in his eye. "Is that so, Teddy?"

Teddy's eyes dropped to the ground, mortified. "Yes, um, yeah, you'll be the first...I'll let you know how it goes, whenever it goes." What was up with him? This was why I preferred that people not talk so much about us getting married. It put a lot of undue pressure on Teddy when maybe he wasn't ready. Unfortunately, a little disappointment still burrowed into my heart. Was it wrong for me to *want* him to be ready?

"I can live with that. Well," he straightened up and gave the counter a little slap. "I won't hold you any longer. I heard there's someone special coming to visit you."

I wrinkled my brow, rocking Junior for no particular reason at all. "Waiting for me? Are we expecting somebody, honey?" I looked to Teddy, who blushed furiously and glared at the ground. I panicked, just a little bit. "Is this somebody we don't want to see?"

Teddy's eyes met mine just for a second, then he dropped them back to the floor again, studying the hell out of the gray-streaked white linoleum. "What? No, you'll be happy, I promise."

"Then why do you look so upset?"

"Uhh…"

Just then, a shout rang out from the other end of the hallway. Everybody stopped dead to look toward the sound.

"Dr. Chalmers! Nurse Teddy!" It was Delores in a green soccer uniform, pumping her legs as she ran toward us full speed. The beads in her braided hair made little clicks with every footfall.

I gasped. I hadn't seen her since her surgery a year ago. Not only was she surviving, she was thriving. Running and everything. "Look at her go." Teddy laid a comforting hand on my shoulder, sniffling as he held back tears. I handed Junior back to him, just for a second. We did the "baby handoff shuffle" again, but Junior didn't mind; he'd conked out about two minutes after getting settled against my chest.

Delores ran toward me, her little tennis shoes slapping on the hospital floor. I crouched down and opened my arms and she ran into them, giving me a big hug. "Hi Dr. Chalmers! Thank you for putting my heart back in after you fixed it!"

I laughed out loud. "I never took it out, kiddo. We fixed it while it was still inside you. That's why we put you to sleep, so it wouldn't hurt while we fixed it."

She stuck a finger in her mouth and chewed. "Oh. I thought you had to put me to sleep and take it out so you could send it to get fixed like in the toy store."

"No way, princess. Otherwise you would have looked like a big ol' Frankenstein."

Delores shook her head, making her braids swing and her beads click. "No, I don't wanna look like Frankenstein. Unless it's Halloween. But after that, still no. I wanna look like The Joker."

"No Bane anymore?" Teddy asked incredulously. He almost sounded sad. The past year had truly flown by.

Delores chewed on her finger a little more, tilting her head as she thought it over. "No. Bane was cool, but I'm really starting to appreciate The Joker as a pure psychopath and agent of chaos." Teddy and I looked at each other, both of our faces saying, *huh?!*

"Kids say the darndest things, right?" Teddy said, his face still crumpled in confusion.

Delores forgot all about evil villains and looked at me with a bright smile again. "Thanks for fixing my heart without sending it to the repair shop, Doctor Chris!" She threw herself around Teddy's legs, squeezing tight. "Thank you, Nurse Teddy, for always being there when I needed you."

Teddy rubbed her back with the hand that wasn't holding our little bundle, his voice thick with tears. "You're welcome, little lady. I'm so glad to see you up and running, literally."

She pulled at her soccer shirt with both hands and held out

the shiny emerald-colored material to show the little mascot, a horned goat. "Oh, that's all I do now. It's my job."

I chuckled. "I bet you're awesome at it."

Rhonda and James came down the hall at a much slower pace, but they weren't far behind.

Rhonda squeezed Teddy as much as possible around the baby in his arms. "There he is, the best nurse on planet Earth."

James gave me a huge, back-slapping hug. "Hey, doc. Congratulations on your first surgery back. I hear it was a huge success. I hear you've had success with a few other things, too." He tilted his head toward Teddy and Junior.

"You can say that again." I stroked Junior's cheek with a couple of fingers, leaning against my alpha's shoulder. "The two loves of my life," I cooed.

Delores looked up at Junior with wide, curious eyes, so I crouched down in front of her.

"Hey sweetie, you wanna meet somebody very special?" She nodded fast, as quiet as I had ever seen her. "Remember a long time ago, right before we did your surgery, you said you wanted me to bring you something? Or should I say, someone?" She nodded faster. "To be more specific, you wanted me and Teddy to bring you someone. At the time, I didn't even know who Teddy was. I thought you were talking about a stuffed animal."

Delores grinned then. "Yeah, but I was talking about Nurse Teddy. He's not a stuffed animal. He's a very handsome man." James, Rhonda, and I burst into a shocked laugh. Teddy, on the other hand, turned beet red and dropped his chin to hide his face.

"You're right, honey," I said through the laughter, "Teddy is a *very* handsome man. He's no stuffed animal, but he sure is fun to squeeze."

"Oh, god," Teddy muttered, burying his face in his free hand, blushing furiously, but smiling in the bashful way he did when I flirted with him.

I smirked at James and Rhonda, who were loving it. "That never gets old." I gripped Delores' little shoulders, giving them a light squeeze. "We did have a baby, after all. His name is Theodore Behrens, Junior and he's the cutest little guy in the world. You know what? You made that wish for us, and it came true. Junior is our miracle wish baby, and we want you to meet him. If you sit down and hold really still, you can hold him."

"Yes, yes, yes, I wanna hold him!" Delores scampered for the nearest seat, which just so happened to be a rolling chair that one of the medical assistants had temporarily vacated. The wheels rattled a little as she climbed in and sat down. She sat up straight and crossed her ankles, staying in place but vibrating with energy. The hallway and nurses' station buzzed with staff and people visiting patients, most of whom were slowing down to stare and grin at the adorable scene.

"We'll make sure the chair doesn't go anywhere, and we can get a good look at Junior while we're at it," Rhonda said as she and James took up positions behind the chair, Rhonda's hand on Delores' thin shoulder.

"Hold out your arms like this." I made a hoop shape to show her what to do. "Mostly he's gonna be on your legs, but you gotta keep your arms still so you can support his head. He's too little to hold it up on his own so he needs your help with that. Show us how strong you are. Okay?"

"Okay!" Delores nodded, eager and focused and making a hoop with her arms.

Teddy lowered Junior down carefully, still holding most of his weight as he settled our son into Delores' lap.

"One arm under his legs like that," he said, as patient and gentle as always. "The other under his head like that. Very good,

Delores." Teddy dropped to one knee in front of her, tucking his hands under her elbows for extra support. Delores had been through a lot and was such a spunky and precocious kid it was easy to forget how young she was. In that moment, though, she radiated innocent, childish joy like the five-year-old little girl she was.

Junior didn't seem to care one way or the other. He was dead set on getting his sleep, his eyes closed and his tiny mouth slightly parted, his little chest rising and falling in what seemed like impossibly quick breaths, but it was just that his lungs were so little they didn't need much air.

Delores twisted her head to her mom and dad, who leaned in close to appreciate the heartwarming scene. "See, I said! I said they were gonna bring me their baby! Well, I came to them, but I was right!"

Teddy nodded in agreement. "You were right, sweetheart. You all were." He lifted his eyebrows towards Rhonda and James. "Thanks for putting the idea in my head. I never in a million years would have thought I could get with an omega like Chris. He's so far out of my league." It seemed like he would never stop saying those things that made me feel like some kind of star.

James tapped him on he shoulder. "I think you both won, my friend."

"I think *I* won. I got a baby out of the deal," Delores said, looking down at Junior with fierce pride on her face as we chuckled around her. Her big, curious eyes lifted to mine. "How did you do it, anyway?"

"How did I do it? You mean where did he come from? Well, he was born four months ago. He was in my tummy in the time I didn't see you."

"He really is cute."

"I think so, yeah."

Her starry eyes sparkled hopefully. "Can I keep him?"

Teddy piped up. "How about if we let you borrow him sometimes?"

I nodded along. "That would be really helpful if your mom and dad wanted to *borrow* him every now and again."

Rhonda leaned over, stroking Junior's hand with a finger. "You got it. We'll *borrow* him whenever you need us to."

I pumped my fist. "Babysitters we love and trust. Score."

Delores squinted at me. "Hey. You said he was in your tummy, like, you had to grow him there. How did he get in there?" All of the adults went silent, looking from right to left, at a loss for words. Delores had another epiphany. "He had to come out of your tummy somehow. How did he come out? Did you have surgery, too?"

I grimaced. "Uh, I don't think I'm the right one to talk to you about that, dear."

"Why not? You're a doctor." Teddy ducked his head as he cracked up.

"That's true, but I'm not a baby doctor."

Her little face scrunched. "Yeah, you are. You're a doctor for little kids and babies."

I slid a hand down my face. "Oh boy, I'm not helping my cause, am I?"

James jumped in, patting Delores' shoulder, smiling but with gritted teeth. "We'll talk about it later, baby. I'm not gonna like it, but we'll talk about it."

Teddy squeezed Delores elbow, thankfully changing the subject. "You and I still have that important thing to do, remember?" Delores gave another quick, bright-eyed nod as James came around the chair to pick Teddy up from her lap. "Are you still gonna be my big helper?"

Delores gave him a very serious, very sharp salute, which was hilarious considering how small she was, and shouted, "Aye, aye, captain!" I covered my mouth with my hand to hide my smile.

"That's just great, sweetie. You have the surprise with you?"

"Yup," Delores said, bouncing in the chair, making it squeak and roll a couple of centimeters. "But you gotta do the thing, though, right? The knee thing."

"What knee thing?" I asked. I was so lost. What surprise would Teddy have Delores help him with that he didn't tell me about?

It hit me then. The "knee thing" was a proposal. Rhonda and James were giddy behind me, and now that I was paying attention, it was obvious they'd been anticipating something big. At that moment, Jing appeared far down the hall, her arms crossed as she strolled closer, taking in the scene with a proud smile. She knew, too, the sneak.

My mouth hung open as Teddy went down on one knee in front of me, shaking like a leaf, but his lips pressed together with determination. He waved Delores over and helped her sit on the propped-up knee. Time stopped. Everyone around us was frozen, watching, beaming with excitement.

"No wonder you're even more shy than normal," I whispered. "You looked scared to death."

"Mm-hm," he said, "I am, but it's not gonna stop me from having you." Chills went down my spine. "Hit it, Delores."

Delores pulled a folded piece of paper from her pocket. She read in her outdoor voice, with her little chest poked out with confidence.

"Dear Chris, I have been wanting to ask you this for a very long time. I knew when I first heard your name that you were somebody special, but I had no idea that I would meet you, let alone…let alone get to know you, then fall in love with you. What we have is sackered..sack-red…"

"Say-cred," Teddy whispered in her ear.

"Sacred," she said with a nod. "And I would not have it any other way. As a matter of fact, I want to have it this way forever. You are the best doctor because you know how to fix anybody's heart, even five-year-olds who love soccer." Delores dropped her voice to a whisper. "I added that part myself. It's true, though." I laughed, even though my throat was thick with emotion. "I want to spend the rest of my life showing you how special you are. Will you do me the ho-" she hesitated, "hoh-nore?"

Teddy whispered in her ear. "Ah-ner."

"Oh. Will you do me the honor of being my husband?" She looked at Teddy. "Was that good?"

Teddy patted her shoulder as onlookers whooped and clapped. "It was perfect, Delores. Great job."

She whispered to Rhonda, as if we couldn't hear her, "Momma, do you have my box?"

"Sure do." Rhonda handed it to her. It wasn't what I expected. It wasn't small enough to be a ring box. It was closer to the size of about three CD cases stacked on top of each other. It was fancy, though. Gold and glittering.

Oh. *Oh.* Milk chocolate truffles with a honey center. The same candies I bid on to win my alpha. Delores opened the top, and there, nestled in the center of a bed of decadent chocolates, was a ring. I forgot how to breathe. Time slowed down around me.

Two of the candy spaces were empty.

"Delores," Rhonda hissed.

"What? They were *good.*" Teddy and I dissolved into laughter, which put both of us at ease. After all, getting engaged didn't have to be all formal and scary. It could be like every other part of our relationship; sweet, intimate, easy.

Teddy cleared his throat, shifting a little on his one knee, that probably hurt on the unforgiving floor. He wrapped his arm tighter around Delores' midsection, bracing for my answer. "So. Chris. Will you?"

Delores bounced on his knee, clapping her little hands. "Yeah, will you?"

The words burst out of my mouth. "The answer is yes. Yes, I'll marry you, Nurse Teddy Bear."

Teddy was shocked. "You will?"

I really laughed at that. "Did you think I was gonna say no?"

"Well, uh, no, I just…are you sure?"

"Teddy, get up here." He lifted Delores off his knee and onto her feet. I grabbed both his hands and pulled him so he stood in front on me, face-to-face, heart-to-heart. I bounced on the balls of my feet, so excited I could flap my arms and take off like a propellor plane. "Put it on, hurry up!" Reverently, Teddy slid the honey-gold band onto my finger. It fit perfectly.

I threw my arm around his neck and kissed my alpha, now my fiancé, hard and sloppy. I forgot anyone else was even around. All I knew was, *I'm marrying the alpha I love. He wants me for the rest of my life. He's mine forever.* Teddy kissed me back with that burning intensity he'd released since our first night together. It was ten times hotter this time, fueled by the surprise and the adrenaline and the pure, bright joy of the moment. Bystanders were really clapping and cheering now, but as thrilled as I was that so many people I cared about saw me pledge my life to my alpha, all I saw was him.

"Gross!" Delores yelled behind us. She slapped her hands over her eyes in her usual dramatic fashion. "I'm too little to see *this.*"

Reluctantly, I untangled my tongue from Teddy's as Delores' parents leaned on each other, wheeze-laughing, Junior wriggling a little in irritation, probably wondering what all this commotion was disturbing his sleep.

I giggled. "Uh oh, we're in public."

"I don't care," he said, chasing my mouth even though he was flushing high on his rosy cheeks.

I cradled his cheek, mumbling against his lips. "You caught me totally off guard, you know that?"

He kissed me again. "I did?"

"I thought you didn't like what Dr. Gupta said earlier because you weren't ready to get married."

"Shucks, honey, I would have married you after like, our third date. I didn't want to scare you to death. You liked it, though, right, the proposal? You're happy?"

"'Did I like it,' he says. 'Am I happy,' he says." I kissed him again, and it seemed like we were having our own little contest to see who could steal more kisses from the other.

"At this rate you'll have another one in no time," James teased, gently patting Junior's round belly.

"We're working on it," Teddy replied, planting another kiss on my cheek.

"So *that's* how babies are made!" Delores yelled, pointing at us and making a "yuck" face. "With lots of gross kissing! I'm never gonna do that. No babies for me."

James pretended to wipe his brow with his free hand. "Phew."

Rhonda snorted. "Just wait until puberty hits, it'll be a whole different story."

"I'm not ready."

Rhonda nodded at us. "We get to see it, thanks to the two of you. Now, go on, have your happily ever after."

I wanted my happily ever after to start horizontally, but we were far, far away from a bed. I looked back and forth, trying to find a broom closet, something, anything. "We gotta find somebody to take the baby so we can-" My eyes dropped down to Delores, looking at me expectantly. "You know."

"We can keep Junior for a while if the two of you need a little *privacy*," James teased.

"Would you mind?" Teddy asked hopefully.

"We're always happy to help. We know the struggle of finding alone time when you have a little one. On top of that, we value the both of you so much and want you to celebrate your engagement and be happy."

"Really?"

"Yes. Definitely. No doubt about it."

I poked Teddy in the shoulder, grinning. "Go get his baby bag before they change their minds." Teddy took a couple of steps, but then he seemed to remember something. He wrapped me up in his arms and gazed at me with an intensity I'd never seen from him. It cut right to the heart of me.

"What is it, baby?" I asked, breathlessly.

"I'm so grateful you were the first person I ever kissed. You're the only person I ever want to kiss. I wanna kiss you with my very last breath, then I can leave this earth a happy alpha."

My heart fluttered and thumped, my belly swooped and my knees buckled. That would never change with Teddy as my alpha.

I laid a hand on his chest, working my fingertips beneath the collar of his shirt. "You know, you're pretty smooth when you really want to be."

He shrugged. That bashful grin I loved was plastered all over his face, looking lovestruck over me, and wasn't it special to be loved by Teddy Behrens? "What can I say, baby? Just being honest."

"Keep it up."

"I will, honey. Forever. Always." We sealed it with a kiss.

***

Want to read more by Ava? Check out His Protective Alpha, on sale now!

Also, get a FREE shortstory! Sign up for my newsletter!

FREE SHORTS WHEN YOU JOIN MY NEWSLETTER!

Loved the story? Please REVIEW!

Hi, my lovely reader! If you loved the book, can you do me a favor and leave a review? It spreads the word and lets other readers know they're getting something they'll love.

You can find all my books on my Amazon author page!

FREE short story! Sign up for my newsletter!

Want a funny, sweet story that introduces you to the men of Primrose Keep? Of course you do! Sign up for my newsletter and get it FREE!

Thanks for being awesome!

NEED MORE AVA?

Read the rest of the Bake Sale Bachelors series!

Book One: Salted Caramel Chaos by Jena Wade
Book Two: Lollipop Lovin' by Lorelei M. Hart
Book Three: Marzipan Magic by Leyla Hunt
Book Four: Marshmallow Madness by Colbie Dunbar
Book Five: Maple Sugar Mix-up by Kallie Frost

More books by Ava

Omega Holidays:
Book One: His Accidental Christmas Omega (Shane and Drew)
Book Two: His Accidental Valentine's Omega (Mitch and Jeremiah)
Book Three: His Accidental Shamrock Omega (Kellen and Lucky)

Omega Mansion:

Prequel: Omega in the House! (Parker and Scott)
Book One: Tearing Down His Omega Walls (Alex and Beckett)
Book Two: His Omega Anchor (Miguel and Hunter)
Book Three: Accepting His Omega's Baby (Jordan and Taylor)

Seven Corners Shifters:
Book One: His Protective Alpha (Bronx and Rashad)
Book Two: A Chance With His Alpha (Tris and Channarong)
Book Three: The Fox's Reluctant Alpha (Jorik and Duncan)

Keeper Omegas:
Book One: This Omega's A Keeper! (Ace and Cassidy)
Book Two: His Omega's Safe Keeper (Jock and Bubbles)

Omegas In Bloom:
Book One: Fresh as a Daisy Omega (Colby and Preston)

Omega Co-ed Standalone:
His Secret Omega Co-ed (Cody and Grayson)